FLORIDA FLING

DEBBIE WHITE

KDP B07PG36V9F 978-1091161955

Ingram Spark ISBN 978-1-955315-07-4

FLORIDA FLING

Editing by Kerry Genova, writersresourceinc.com

&

Leo Bricker, Grammatical Eye®

Cover Design by Larry White

*R*uby tossed the Frisbee into the air and watched as Red ran and jumped, catching the blue disc in midair.

"Come here, boy. Bring it to Mommy."

Red galloped up to Ruby but at the last minute dodged her hands, and with the Frisbee still in his mouth, shot past her, kicking up sand as he sped by.

"You rascal," she called out, laughing at his silliness.

He raced down the shoreline, braked to a screeching halt, turned without any notice and came running full steam ahead, only to stop quickly at her feet. Globs of gooey salvia oozed out of the sides of his mouth as he held on to the Frisbee.

Ruby reached down and retrieved the Frisbee. Looking at the slobber on her hand, she crinkled up her nose. "Ooh. Yuck." She untied the bandanna from around his neck and used it to clean her hands. "You crazy boy," she said as she patted him on the head, getting sprayed by saliva with his flailing tongue. "You need water."

Red dashed along beside Ruby, leaping as he nipped at the Frisbee while the two trudged through the sand to home. The weather-beaten wood creaked as she sprinted up to the deck level of the cottage. A bowl of water awaited Red. He immediately began to lap it up, sloshing water everywhere. Ruby put her hands on her hips and blew out a breath. Shaking her head, she smiled as she watched him make a mess.

Her life had changed so much after she rescued him. An Irish Setter, Red's mahogany coat, lean frame, and carefree spirit made him quite a striking companion. No one saw the potential but Ruby. With ribs showing from malnutrition and his fur knotted to the skin, nails way too long and teeth requiring a good cleaning, he was overlooked too many times as a potential pet. Most people were looking for lap dogs. This energetic boy would need lots of exercise. One look into his soulful eyes and she knew she had to bring him home. It was during one night sitting on the porch, listening to the seagulls flap and squawk overhead, when she decided what to name him. Red seemed the perfect name and was symbolic with her own, Ruby.

If it hadn't been for Red's continued companionship, Ruby would be all alone. Sure, she had friends, but being an author sometimes meant being alone more than being around people. She had to keep focused on her writing which meant long hours with just her thoughts and the computer. And don't get her started on men. That was a joke. She'd tried dating, but no man had the confidence necessary to compete with her and her daunting schedule. It never failed; they'd become obsessive, compulsive, and in the end, they'd walk away saying she cared more about writing than she did about them. They might be right. And in the rare instances they hadn't ended it, she had. There was only so much neediness one could handle. If her grandmother were alive, she'd tell Ruby it was because the right guy hadn't come along. She reached over and scratched Red behind the ears. She longed to find someone like one of her characters in her books. She always wrote the perfect book boyfriend.

She slipped her hand in her back pocket and pulled out her phone. "Hey, Red. It's time for our visit to Shady

Grove Place. Let me run a brush through your fur and get you freshened up."

RED LEAPED into the front seat of her bright yellow VW bug with green flowers plastered on the bumper. He sat as she crossed around to the driver's side. A hint of a grin washed across her lips as she slipped inside the car. Red wagged his tail rapidly, causing a slapping noise against the car door, his excitement for a car ride with his mommy apparent.

"Good boy, Red. Settle down," Ruby said, patting him on the head.

She gave herself a quick look in the rearview mirror while she started up the car. It sputtered and rattled, and a puff of smoke shot out of the tailpipe causing Red to whine. People in Shady Grove were used to seeing her car with Red in it. Once a town with a few thousand or more residents, Shady Grove was now a vacation paradise occupied by tourists wanting a slice of heaven, or local weekenders enjoying their properties. In the summertime, it was a busy little resort town, but many times it was just Ruby and Red having the entire shoreline to themselves. Shady Grove Place, a retirement community, was about an hour and forty minutes from Orlando, making city life close by. Over the narrow bridge from Shady Grove, smaller communities offering services such as medical, fire, and police, not to mention shopping, made going all the way to Orlando just a once in a while thing. Ruby had everything she needed right here in Shady Grove. Or so she thought.

She steered the car into the parking lot. "Here we are."

As they passed the reception desk, Ruby waved to Mrs. Parker. She'd been running the desk for as long as Ruby could remember. She often joked with Ruby that she'd go from being an employee to a resident one of these days.

"They've been waiting for you," Mrs. Parker said.

Ruby and Red made their way to the large living room where an old, upright, out of tune piano sat in one corner, a couple of couches and some chairs—all mismatched—lining the walls. A coffee table with stacks of magazines and a bookcase filled with books and puzzles made up the rest of the furniture.

Red made sure he got a pat on the head from each of the residents in the living room as they made their way to the small outdoor patio area where they found more folks enjoying the sunshine. Mr. Carrolton beamed when it was his turn to visit with Red and Ruby.

"Good day, missy," the old man said.

"Hello, Mr. Carrolton. How are you today?" Ruby pulled up a chair and sat.

"I can't complain. It wouldn't help if I did." He chuckled.

This was his standard line whenever she asked him how he was doing. "Well, I'm glad to hear that," she said.

"Did you hear the news?" He combed his fingers through Red's wavy fur.

Ruby tilted her head. "What news is that?"

"They're giving us the boot."

She wrinkled her brows.

"Closing down the place. We have until the end of the year to find a new place to live."

Ruby gulped. "Seriously? What brought that about?"

"The city thinks we're not habitable."

"That's ridiculous." She looked around at the concrete with large cracks, the swimming pool that hadn't been used for years because it had leaks, and when her gaze traveled up, she saw chipped paint and dry-rotted wood on the old building. She sighed.

"My son wants me to move in with him. But I just hate to be a burden."

"I'm sure you wouldn't be a burden, Mr. Carrolton. But I understand your desire to be independent."

"As independent as I can be. He's a little upset with the way they've let this place go. When I first moved in, this was a palace." He grunted.

"I agree it could use some TLC. I guess I never really paid attention. What does Mrs. Parker say about it?"

"She said she talked to the owners, but they are having financial difficulties, and apparently many of the residents here are not paying their rent. Makes it difficult to make improvements if they aren't getting their rent money."

Ruby twisted her mouth tightly while thumping her cheek with her finger. "There's got to be something we can do."

"Several of the residents have already moved. We're down to about twenty of us now."

Ruby stood. "Let me see what I can do. I can't promise to change the mind of the city, but maybe I can get us some more time."

Mr. Carrolton stood and began to take a few wobbly steps.

"Are you okay?" Ruby took his arm to steady him.

"Yeah. It's just that darn arthritis. If I sit too long, I'm stiff as a board."

She held on to his elbow as he shuffled in. When they got inside, he gave her a backhanded wave and told Red goodbye. Ruby watched him as he slowly made his way down the hall to his efficiency apartment.

Ruby walked over to the reception desk. She studied the peeling wallpaper. "Mrs. Parker, Mr. Carrolton just told me the news. Is there anything we can do?"

"I don't know, dear. Rumor has it that one of the family members of one of the residents is stirring the pot to make this happen." She nodded toward the hall.

Ruby looked where she motioned. Mr. Carrolton was just turning the corner of the hall. "Mr. Carrolton's son?"

"It's all speculation, but I have it on good authority to be true," Mrs. Parker said.

"Why would he do that?"

"He wants Joel to move to Orlando."

"But Joel—Mr. Carrolton wants to live here. He loves his independence."

"I know. But look around. He has a valid concern." Mrs. Parker tipped her head toward the overhead light fixtures with missing bulbs.

"I know. We just need to refresh this place. Get it up to the standards as it should be. Can you please give me the telephone number to the owners? I'm going to call them."

Mrs. Parker scribbled something down and handed Ruby a piece of paper. "They're really nice folks. I think they are probably in over their heads with this project."

Ruby scratched her head. "Mr. Carrolton told me that many of the folks here aren't paying their rent. That's part of the issue."

"He's accurate. And you want to know why they aren't paying?" She didn't give Ruby an opportunity to answer. "They are demanding certain things before they pay."

Ruby cocked her head. "Oh?"

Mrs. Parker rested her arms on the counter. She motioned for Ruby to come closer. Ruby let out a short burst of air from her lungs. Most of the people who lived there were hard of hearing. She leaned in.

"They want the swimming pool repaired, new carpet in their apartments, and the dining room open again."

"These requests don't seem unreasonable, Mrs. Parker."

"And to top that off, the owners haven't paid the property taxes in two years. The state has put a lien against the place."

Ruby crossed her arms. "And it just keeps getting better."

"Yep. Lots of issues."

"Okay, well I'm going to contact them." Her gaze dropped to the small piece of paper.

"Good luck," Mrs. Parker said.

"Come on, Red. We've got some work to do."

AFTER A DINNER OF CRACKERS, cheese, and salami, Ruby took her glass of wine out on the back porch so she could enjoy the sunset and hear the waves. Red curled up on his well-worn dog bed and snored softly. Rocking in her chair, she tossed around what she was going to say to the owners of Shady Grove Place. With every start, she shook her head. "That sounds condescending, Ruby." She'd start again. "Nope. That isn't going to work." She picked up the cell phone and studied it. Maybe the words would flow when she heard their voice? She punched in the numbers and slowly put the phone to her ear. It rang three times before a voice answered.

"Hello," a man's voice bellowed, making Ruby pull the phone away.

She swallowed hard, then placed the phone to her ear. "Hello," she said her voice barely above a whisper. "My name is Ruby Bennett."

"We don't want any. Take us off your list," he screamed.

"No, wait. I'm not soliciting anything." That wasn't completely true. "I visit your assisted living center with my dog Red. I've been going there for many years."

Silence.

"I'm calling because I'm concerned about Mr. Carrolton and all the residents."

More silence.

"Hello. Can you hear me?"

"I can hear you. There's nothing we can do. We're filing bankruptcy."

"Are you sure there's nothing we can do?" Ruby pleaded.

"Thanks to Joel's son," the man said. "He's the one you can thank."

Ruby gulped the air down her throat before speaking. "I understand he does have some concern, and I'll reach out to him as well. But I wanted to see what we could do first."

"Because of him pointing out all the things wrong here, the remaining residents are all in a huff about repairs. They're holding my rent hostage until I make them. I can't afford to make expensive repairs without my rent money coming in. There are taxes to be paid, utilities, not to mention Mrs. Parker's salary."

Ruby paused a moment to gather her thoughts. This was indeed a sensitive issue. "Mrs. Parker mentioned something about back taxes."

"Oh, that Mrs. Parker—she can't keep anything under wraps. Yes, I owe back taxes, but I'm in constant communication with the city. I'm working on getting an extension. It just hasn't come through yet."

"How much do you owe?"

"Twelve thousand dollars."

"Okay. So that's the first thing that should be paid. We could have a fund-raiser. We could try and earn that."

"The town of Shady Grove don't care about the old folks. They want a gas station," the man said.

"I have an idea. Can you meet me at Shady Grove Place tomorrow? Say around noon?"

"I can, won't be of any use. It will cost too much money to get Shady Grove Place up to standards."

"Mr. Jensen, don't give up just yet. See you tomorrow."

CHAPTER 2

That night while Ruby nibbled on dinner, she made a list of what she would like to see happen at Shady Grove Place. Her mind raced as she jotted down the items. She should be finishing her romance novel, not saving an old folks' home!

Ruby made her living as a romance writer. She'd always loved to write, so after finishing college at a nearby liberal arts school, she made a trip to see her grandmother in Shady Grove. It was just supposed to be for a few weeks while she unwound from the rigorous college itinerary she'd endured for the past four years. But a couple of weeks turned into a couple of months, and after she'd written her first book and the royalties came floating in, she never looked back. Then her grandmother passed away and left her the cottage.

She peeped over at Red. He was lying with both feet out and his head resting on them. "What's wrong, Red?" She scooted her chair out and stood. Red perked up and trotted over to her. She leaned over and patted him on the head, then ran her hand down his back, giving him a quick massage. He yawned, then moseyed back over to his bed. She shrugged and turned back to her list.

Satisfied she'd done all she could do, she opened her laptop and plonked out a chapter before heading to bed. Living on the beach did many things for her, but the one thing it did best, it gave her great inspiration for her novels.

She headed off to bed feeling a bit anxious about tomorrow's meeting with Mr. Jensen.

"GOOD AFTERNOON, RUBY," Mrs. Parker said. "What brings you back so soon?" She leaned her elbows on the counter.

Ruby walked over to her as she scoured the room for Mr. Jensen. She had no idea what he looked like, but she did know the residents. "I'm waiting for Mr. Jensen."

Mrs. Parker reared back, and with a look of sheer horror, covered her mouth.

"Now, now, Mrs. Parker. Don't get so excited."

She came closer to the desk. "He's meeting you here?"

Ruby nodded.

"Well, he's not here yet. Let me put on some coffee and spruce up the living room." She jogged around from the front desk, waving a dust rag. She rushed to the tables and bookshelves and ran the cloth along the wood. Ruby looked on. After she did the quickest dusting job Ruby had ever witnessed, she hurriedly made her way back to the office, presumably making coffee.

Ruby chuckled. *When the boss comes visiting everyone jumps through hoops.*

"I wish someone told me he was coming," Mrs. Parker yelled out from the back room.

"Why?" Ruby yelled back.

"I'd have made sure we had pastries or something."

Ruby shook her head as she moved away. A man came waltzing through the front door, causing her to look. He was probably in his mid to late sixties. Average build, bald, wearing tan Dockers and a blue polo shirt tucked in. He was actually in pretty good shape. She followed him with her gaze as he came closer.

"You must be Ruby Bennett?" He held out his hand.

"It's nice to meet you, Mr. Jensen." She gazed past him toward the sofa along the wall. "Why don't we go over here and talk."

"Hello, Mr. Jensen," Mrs. Parker called out. "I just made a fresh pot of coffee. Would you like some?"

"Sounds great, Hazel. Cream, please." He moved away from the counter and led the way to the couch.

"Hazel? I just know her as Mrs. Parker."

He crossed his legs. "Yes, Hazel has worked here at Shady Grove Place for a very long time."

Mrs. Parker brought the coffee. Ruby watched as she set the cup down before him. Mr. Jensen cleared his throat to get Mrs. Parker's attention.

Her gaze shifted from him to Ruby. "Oh, I'm sorry. Would you like a cup too?" Mrs. Parker said.

"Thank you. Cream, please," Ruby replied.

Mrs. Parker hurried off to get Ruby her cup of coffee.

'I've been coming to Shady Grove Place now for about ten years. I started visiting here with my grandmother. She had a dear friend who lived here. Apartment number 8. I remember it so well," Ruby said.

"Ten years, huh?" He brought the cup of coffee to his lips and tasted it.

"I've become friends with most of the residents here. I bring my dog, Red," she said looking over toward Red, smiling. "It helps for the old people to see friendly faces, and they love Red."

The man tipped his head up and down. "So why did you ask me to come here? So you can tell me how the residents love your smiling face?"

Ruby's face tightened as a wave of anger washed over her. "No, I asked you to come here because I have some ideas on how we can save Shady Grove Place and not have it become a gas station." She crossed her arms.

"I'm listening."

"I think a fund-raiser could be the key here. I'd like to see us do some sort of event. A few actually. We'd open it up to the people of Shady Grove to get them to come and see what is at stake here. I'd drum up some music, food, and I'd be happy to donate my time and whatever else to make this a success."

"You haven't said how, though. What's it going to cost me?"

"I can get back to you with costs, but I'd like to see what I can get people to volunteer and donate first. I know you have a deadline when those taxes must be paid. What is it?"

The man sat his cup down and folded his arms across his lap. "Three weeks from today. It's not enough time, I'm afraid."

"At least let me try," Ruby pleaded.

The man stood, straightening his shirt. "Okay, try as you might. You have my telephone number. Let me know the details." He began to move away from Ruby.

"Sir."

Mr. Jensen stopped.

"Thank you. I have one special friend here as you know. Joel Carrolton. I've…we've been visiting him here for several years. He loves living here. I don't know why his son is doing this, but he really should think twice."

"Look at the place, Ms. Bennett. Would you want your mother or grandmother living here?" He shook his head, then waved goodbye to Mrs. Parker and left the building.

Ruby walked slowly over to Mrs. Parker, with her head hung down. It hadn't gone exactly the way she'd hoped, but it was a start. Mrs. Parker patted her hands as she rested them on the counter. "Now, now, dear. It'll all work out."

Ruby lifted her head. "Funny. My grandmother used to always say that to me." She cupped Mrs. Parker's hand and smiled.

"Your grandmother sounds like a nice person."

"She was. Listen," Ruby said, changing the subject. "Can you give me Joel's son's phone number? I'm sure he's listed as an emergency contact." She viewed Mrs. Parker through half-closed lids.

"I'm not allowed to give out that information," she stated point-blank.

Ruby nodded.

"But if someone just happened to come around the desk, let's say while I was in the little girls' room, and looked into the alphabetized resident records right here in the file drawer, then it wouldn't be giving it out, would it?" She stepped away from the counter and headed toward the door labeled "ladies," gazing over her shoulder once and winking.

Ruby waited until she was behind closed doors, then rushed around the counter and searched the drawer for Joel's file. She scribbled down the son's phone number and quickly wadded it up, slipping it into her pocket. She hurried back around to the opposite side of the counter, coaxing Red to follow her as she exited the building.

With her heart pounding just a bit after the undercover work, Ruby and Red headed to the local yogurt shop where both humans and fur babies were welcomed.

While Red licked his bowl of vanilla, Ruby devoured her salted caramel topped with chopped candy bars all the while debating the best course of action she called Saving Shady Grove Place. As she finished the last spoonful of the delightful treat, a lightbulb turned on in her brain. She jumped from the chair, causing poor Red to alert to her sudden movement by letting out a short bark.

"It's okay, Red. I just had a brilliant idea." She tossed their containers into the trash, bid the store clerk farewell and went on their merry way.

SHE WENT over it in her mind several times before she placed the call. She'd be polite but businesslike. The phone rang in her ear four times when a soft, sexy voice answered.

She stuttered, then identified who she was. "Hi, you don't know me, but my name is Ruby Bennett. I live in Shady Grove. I'm friends with your father, Joel."

"If this is about me wanting to move Dad out of there… I'm doing it for his own safety."

She could feel her cheeks flush. This was harder than she thought it would be. She paced the small living room of the cottage before heading outdoors. The ocean always made her think clearly.

"I totally understand how you feel about it. I don't really find you wrong in your feelings, but thought instead we could try and make things right…for Joel and the rest of the residents."

"Who are you? Some sort of do-gooder, a savior of the less fortunate?" His tone smacked of mockery and made her blood boil.

"No, not really. But I have some ideas on how to save the place. It's so important to Joel and so many of the residents." Her face was not only burning up with anger, but her heart was also beating so fast she could hardly hear herself think.

"I'm sorry. I'm a bit on edge, I think. I could get in a lot of trouble by the state regarding my father."

"How so?"

"By allowing him to live in such conditions. There's a law on the books. It's called elderly abuse. Are you aware of it?" His voice was now steady, but his sentence still pitched with anxiety.

"Yes, I'm aware of that law. But if we do something to fix it, then they'll see our heart is in the right place. Please, just meet with me."

Ruby held her breath as she waited for his answer.

"Okay. I'll stop by after my visit with my dad."

Ruby gave him her address, and feeling pretty optimistic about the call said, "I'll see you tomorrow afternoon, then."

CHAPTER 3

*R*uby had no idea how Joel's son would be, and if the phone conversation hadn't ended on an upbeat, she would have said he was grumpy like Joel could be, but why? He wasn't much older than her. She knew she was fond of Joel. He was such a nice old man despite his grumpy days. She figured he had a right to some complaining, although he rarely did. But he was getting older and over the ten years, she did notice some changes in him.

She made a pitcher of iced tea, set out some cookies, and spruced up the cottage. She brushed Red's thick coat until it was free of knots and shined like new glass, then she spritzed on some dog cologne and finished up his grooming with a new bandanna around his neck. She heard a car drive up and park. A few moments later, a light rap on the screen door.

"Hi. You must be Joel's son, Drake." She extended her hand to him.

When he shook her hand, a jolt of energy came over her. She dismissed it as just nerves and invited him in.

"Care for a glass of iced tea?" She reached for the pitcher.

"That sounds good." He pulled out a chair.

"I thought we could sit outside on the porch. It's a nice day and all." She shrugged, feeling a bit giddy inside.

He pushed the chair back under the table. "Okay." He took the glass from her.

She carried her own glass and the plate of cookies and led the way. She set the plate on the glass top of the old white rattan table and sat. She tipped her chin for him to take a seat.

She stared out into the waves. "Such a beautiful day, isn't it?"

"Yes. Shady Grove is such a neat little island town."

"I came here several years ago and have never left." She turned and gazed into his eyes. Blue. No, green. No, hazel.

"What is it you wanted to talk to me about?" He drew in a taste of his drink.

"First of all, how is your dad?"

"He's good. Cranky as usual."

"That doesn't sound like Mr. Carrolton." She decided to spare Drake details regarding his "bad days."

"He's grumpy because of the housing situation. He doesn't want to move."

Ruby nodded. "Well I don't really blame him, do you?"

"I can't have my father living in a dilapidated building. What would people think of me?" Drake reached for a cookie.

"It's not that bad," she said, her mouth turning down at the corners.

"Again, why the visit?" Drake said in a cool-tempered voice.

"I met with the owners. They need our help. Right now, they are twelve thousand dollars behind in property taxes. If we get that squared away, we can start on the renovations."

"And I suppose you just want me to write them a check?"

"That would be super if you could do that, but no, I was thinking more about having a fund-raiser," she replied with a touch of snark.

"I'm sorry. I just don't see a way out of this except to move Dad. I don't mean to be ungrateful to you. It's the situation."

"I get it. I do. I was very protective of my grandmother. We lived here together until she passed. I'd have done anything for her, and I did. You only want what is best for your dad. But let's just try this. Because you know your dad really doesn't want to move, and if you do care about his feelings, you'd at least try saving the place he loves and has called home for over ten years."

"Okay. What can I do?"

"I was hoping that you might like to sponsor a golf tournament."

"How'd you know I played golf?" He flashed a wide grin at her.

"Your dad told me in conversation one time. I know Orlando has many courses, so what do you think?"

"That could work. What other ideas do you have?" He took another cookie.

"I'm an author. I have many author friends that live in Florida that love to do charity events. I could ask them if they'd like to donate some books, and we could have a book sale and maybe a rummage sale too."

Drake nodded. "That might work. But do you really think we can raise twelve grand? And how long do we have?"

Ruby hung her head low. "Three weeks," she mumbled.

"Three weeks!" he bellowed.

"I know it's not a lot of time, but I think we can do it. You work the golf tournament angle, and I'll get the book thing going. And for the last fund-raiser, I thought we could have a walkathon or maybe a pet walk?"

Drake's gaze fell to where Red was lying. "I don't have a dog."

"Lots of folks do. But I'll think that one over. Right now, we need to get the other two going. So, are you in?" She shifted back, palms out, waiting for his reply.

"I'm in." He casually looked at his wrist. "I better be going."

"Do you need any help in coordinating the golf event?" She followed him down the steps that led to the sandy beach floor.

"I'll get my girlfriend to help me. She's great at these sorts of things."

"Oh. Okay. Sounds good. I look forward to hearing all about it."

"If you don't mind, I'll have her call you. You know, girl to girl stuff."

"That's fine," Ruby said, recognizing the hitch of pain in her voice.

Her gaze followed him as he walked the well-traveled path lined with tall wheat-colored grasses bending in the night breeze. Red followed him halfway, then came trotting back.

~

He jumped into his sports car, quickly glancing in the rearview mirror. A smile turned up on his mouth as he gazed at Red galloping back to Ruby. He started the engine, then popped the clutch, spinning his wheels just for effect and kicking up sand and rock as he tore out. Once he crossed over the bridge and headed to the onramp to the interstate, he activated his cell phone via Bluetooth. It rang a few times, then a sweet voice answered.

"Hey, Chrissy. How about some dinner? I'm on my way back from visiting Dad."

"Ah. Sure, that will be fine."

"Good. I will pick you up in about an hour and a half. Where do you want to go?"

"Let's meet at Quincy's."

"Meet?" he asked.

"Yeah. I…ah…have an errand to run afterward and need to have my car," Chrissy said.

He shrugged, then answered her. "Okay, see you at Quincy's. I have a big favor to ask of you."

"I have something to share with you too," she said.

Then she clicked off, leaving him wondering what she wanted to tell him.

He'd been dating Chrissy for about two months. Things seemed headed in the right direction. He knew they said picking up girls in bars rarely worked out to anything more than a few dates, and truth be told, he didn't really know where he stood with her. She blew hot and cold. Just like tonight. Tonight, she wanted her own car. Next week she'd hound him to death, making him feel like he was suffocating. She seemed to have quite a bit of emotional baggage. But it wasn't easy meeting women. So he'd stay the course and see where it took him.

He turned up the radio, and when a certain song came on, instead of thinking about his upcoming date with Chrissy, Ruby popped into his brain. Her tawny complexion sprinkled with freckles and her shimmering golden locks with just enough red and eyes the color of the ocean, well, she was quite the looker, not to mention her feisty temperament. Guess it went along with the red hair. He shook it off as he changed lanes, passing some slow driver. As he passed the car, he casually looked over. It was someone old like his dad. "Maybe you shouldn't be driving," he said under his breath.

He pulled into Quincy's, and after tucking in his shirt and running his hand through his hair, he made his way to the little pub known to the locals as the watering hole. Drake often wondered why the owner just didn't name it that instead of Quincy's.

He opened the door and narrowed his eyes, adjusting to the modestly lit restaurant. He walked toward the back where they always sat. He knew she was there because he saw her car parked near his. She almost took his breath away with her long, flowing blonde hair tucked behind her ears and draped over her shoulders, big silver hoops hung from her ears, and shiny pink lip gloss sparkled in the dimly lit space. He leaned over and kissed her. "Hey there." He slid over to the opposite side of the table and sat. "You look gorgeous as ever." He winked.

She blushed, then thanked him. "Thanks for meeting me here." She picked up a menu and covered half of her face.

"I'm in the mood for a burger," he said, putting down the glossy bifold.

She gently closed hers and sat it down. "Salad. I think I'll have a grilled chicken salad."

When the server came over, they placed their orders and then clasped hands on the table.

"I have a super big favor to ask of you. I'm helping a friend coordinate a golf tournament as a fund-raiser to help the assisted living place my dad lives in. It's a long shot, but I sort of promised to help. Would you be able to help me get that going? I mean, I would help, and I'll definitely pass the word around at the office, but with my practice and all my clients I have quite a heavy load right now." He took a long drink of his water.

"I hope you don't mind. I ordered drinks for us."

"No, not at all," he said, sensing something didn't seem quite right.

When their drinks arrived, she played around with the fruit that bobbed on the top, finally pulling out the tooth-pick and eating the cherry.

"You mentioned you had something to tell me?" He drew in a taste of the brew she had ordered for him, wiping the foam from his lips with a napkin.

"It can wait."

"Dad was in rare form today. He's really gung-ho on saving Shady Grove Place." He chuckled, then drew in another sip of his beer.

"What exactly is happening to his home?" she asked.

"The owner hasn't paid property taxes, the residents aren't paying their rent, and the place is falling apart. I want to move Dad in with me. I know that'll put a damper on our relationship, but I can always come over to your place." He reached his hands across the table for hers.

She slowly moved her hands into his. They felt icy and not welcoming at all.

"What's wrong, Chrissy?" He pulled his hands back, leaning deep into the chair.

"Here we go. A nice grilled salad for the young lady and a cheeseburger medium rare for the gentleman." The waiter stepped back. "Anything else I can get you?" His gaze turned to Chrissy first, then to Drake.

"We're good," Drake said, his tone steady and matter-of-fact.

She dug a fork into her salad.

"Are you going to tell me what's bothering you?"

Drake didn't have time for games. He'd been around the block a few times. His heart had been broken a couple of times, too, and now that he was in his late thirties, he made a promise that he wouldn't waste any time on any woman that didn't want to invest in the relationship.

He pushed his burger away. "I have a feeling this might be our last dinner?" He peered down at her through half-closed lids.

She put her fork down.

A shiver zipped up his spine, making his body tense and rigid.

"I was hoping we could finish our dinner before this, but yes, Drake, I just want to be friends." She quickly looked away.

He dropped the fork. The utensil shuddered and shook as it came to a standstill.

"I feel like I want to date other people."

"Date other people," he said, shaking his head. "One minute you want space and the next minute you are choking me, and *you* want to see other people." He chuckled.

"Don't be so dramatic, Drake." She picked up her cocktail. "You can date other people too."

"Oh, and when the other people don't work out, we'll come running back to each other. Is that how it will work? I don't think so."

"We could remain as friends with benefits." She batted her lashes as she sipped her drink.

The sharp look he gave her preceeded his terse answer. "No thank you, Chrissy. I don't want to be your friend with or without benefits." He opened his wallet and dumped a few bills onto the table. He slid out of the booth. He hated that she wouldn't even make eye contact with him. Then he whirled around and walked out of Quincy's, vowing never to eat there again.

He sat in his car, letting the anger build. He gripped the steering wheel tightly as the scenario played over in his mind. *Did what happened just really happen*? He inserted the key and started the engine, then he tore out of the parking lot almost as fast as he did out of Ruby's. At Ruby's, he was just showing off his tail feathers like a beautiful peacock. This time it was because he couldn't get the heck out of there fast enough.

CHAPTER 4

*R*uby went to work contacting several of her author buddies. And as she suspected, all of them agreed to donate their books to the great cause. Because time was of the essence, they also agreed to ship the books overnight. Then she went to work organizing the event.

She picked a Saturday to have it, then she designed some cool flyers advertising the event. She went to her own bookshelves and pulled from her inventory of books and began to make a pile. She called the owner, Mr. Jensen and told him of the goings-on. They agreed that whatever money was raised, if not enough to pay the taxes, would go to help residents find other living arrangements. Satisfied that all the i's were dotted and t's crossed, Ruby went to work with the next step.

"HEY, MRS. PARKER," Ruby said, waving.

"Hello. What are you up to?"

"Up to?" Ruby giggled.

"I can see it in your eyes. You're up to something."

"Does the facility have portable tables? You know, the long kind with folding legs?"

Mrs. Parker placed her finger on her chin and thumped it. "Yes! In the shed."

"Lead the way," Ruby said.

Mrs. Parker grabbed a key off the hook and led Ruby to a large outside storage shed. Inside were five folding tables, about two dozen folding chairs, and a huge chalkboard on an easel that would be perfect for advertising the event. Ruby filled Mrs. Parker in on the details.

"What about adding a bake sale to the book sale?" Mrs. Parker said.

Ruby dropped her hands to her side. "That's a great idea. Hmm. Maybe I have one better. Maybe I could get the bakery to donate some baked goods?"

"I'd be happy to bake some brownies or something," Mrs. Parker said, holding one half of a folding table and walking slowly wherever Ruby guided her.

"Are you all right lifting this?" Ruby asked.

Mrs. Parker was in great shape, and Ruby was trying to remember how old she said she was. Was it seventy? No maybe sixty. Sixty isn't old.

"Let me know if it's too much."

With their tongues hanging out, Ruby and Mrs. Parker used their strength to open the folding legs. They tugged until finally, the tables were sitting upright.

"They need a good cleaning," Mrs. Parker said. Then she took off.

Ruby finished by dragging out the remaining tables. With one foot holding down the table, she managed to open it up. Then she went to the other side. She flipped over the table, and when it was standing, started on the next.

Mrs. Parker came out lugging a bucket of water, sloshing it with each step.

"Here, let me help," Ruby called, taking the bucket out of her hands.

"Soap and a little bleach. Should clean these babies right up," Mrs. Parker said.

After all the tables and chairs were cleaned, Ruby told Mrs. Parker she was going to visit the bakery to see about the donated goods.

"Good luck," Mrs. Parker called out as she pitched the dirty water from the bucket.

RUBY CHECKED her face in the rearview mirror. She quickly licked a finger, removing a smudge from her cheek. She then entered the bakery. Mrs. Sternberg happily greeted her when she walked in.

"Ruby Bennett. How are you?" She began to wipe down the glass display case with a white rag.

"I'm well, Mrs. Sternberg. I have a proposition for you." She straightened her back.

"Oh?" She cocked her head.

"I'm trying to save Shady Grove Place."

"That place is a dump. The owners should be ashamed of themselves."

"Well, it's an unfortunate set of circumstances that have led it to its current disrepair, but I have an idea that might save it."

Ruby was delighted that Mrs. Sternberg was totally on board with the idea once it was presented to her. Mrs. Sternberg agreed to donate two dozen cookies and two dozen cupcakes. Happy for the news, Ruby told her when she'd need them. Showing her support of the small bakery, she purchased a slice of carrot cake to go.

She sat in her car and went over things. Books were on the way, tables cleaned and ready, bakery goods ready… the only thing she needed to do was to distribute the flyers. She stopped at the few other businesses in town and dropped off flyers, then went to the post office and taped one near the mailboxes. She went to the police station and spread the news there, drove to the next town, just ten miles away, and dropped a few more off at some local businesses.

By the time she got home she was tired, and she still had to write a chapter before calling it a day, but not before a quick romp on the beach with a certain redhead.

THE FOLLOWING morning as Drake prepared to go into the law practice he shared with three other attorneys, images of Chrissy during the dreaded break-up dinner played havoc in his brain. He couldn't help it. Although he could never see her as a long-term partner, he did have fun with her—especially after she'd partaken of a few glasses of wine. No matter how rocky their relationship was, they always ended up making up, telling each other how sorry they were for their behavior.

He tried to keep up the smiling face but thinking about the previous night's dinner and Chrissy breaking up with him left him anything but happy. Maybe it was all for the best. If he were to be completely honest, all of his past relationships were bombs. None of them were "take home to mom" kind of girls. That's if his mom were still alive. But he did have Joel. Any woman he wanted to spend the rest of his life with would have to meet Joel's approval, and since he was married to Drake's mom, living up to her might be a bit of a challenge.

Drake decided that telling anyone about the details regarding "no more Chrissy," helped no one and it just dredged up feelings. Feelings he'd just as soon toss aside. So he put his head down and went to work, and before he realized it, it was noon.

Over a tuna sandwich from the cafeteria downstairs, he was soon joined by his partners where they discussed upcoming vacations, babies on the way, and buying a new home. Drake was the youngest partner and all these topics, except the vacation one, were not on his radar. Besides, he had to coordinate a golf tournament.

"I need your help, guys." He took a bite of his sandwich.

All eyes were on him.

"I'm trying to get a golf tournament together for a fundraiser. Can you help a guy out?" He laughed.

They all nodded.

"Great. I have a call in to the Green Valley Golf Course. I should know if they'll accommodate us on the day of. Having your support means a lot. It's to help Shady Grove Place where my dad is living."

"You can count on us," Skip, the senior partner, said.

Roger, the other partner, nodded. "I can ask around too."

"That would be awesome."

LATER THAT DAY, Drake had a message on his phone from Green Valley. They penciled him in for his date. All they required was a deposit.

He dialed Ruby's number.

"Hello?"

He drew in a slow breath. Her sweet voice hummed in his ears. "Hey. This is Drake. How are you?"

"I'm fine. How is the golf tournament planning going? Does your girlfriend need any help?"

Drake swallowed the lump that caught in his throat. "No, she…ah, well, I'm getting it all scheduled."

"Oh. I thought she was going to help you out?"

Drake offered a wobbly smile. Was she digging or was she genuinely caring?

"Yeah, I thought so too. But we're not really seeing each other anymore."

"What? It was just two days ago that you called her your girlfriend," Ruby said, her voice climbing an octave.

"Yeah, that's how I roll. I have a girlfriend one minute, and the next I'm single again." He tried to laugh it off, but he was still kind of hurt.

"I'm sorry. Guess it wasn't meant to be? That's what my grandmother always said when something didn't work out."

"I suppose. Anyway, I don't want to talk about her anymore. She's history. But I do have some exciting news about the tournament."

After he explained how far he'd gotten in coordinating the event, she filled his ear about the book and bake sale.

"Based on preliminary numbers, it looks like we'll be close to the twelve-thousand-dollar mark. But we must do a couple more things to cinch it," Ruby said.

"Maybe ask Mr. Jensen if he can pay anything toward the taxes. Any amount would help," Drake said.

"Done. I'll call him right after I get off the phone with you," Ruby said.

"What about the pet walk idea?" Drake said.

"I think it would work well. I wondered about contacting a few food trucks and have them down on the beach. We could have a Frisbee contest for the dogs, and I could sell bandannas at a booth. People love to dress up their pooches."

Drake cracked a smile. He'd seen some of these pooches dressed up. Some people were just plain crazy, prancing their animals around in outfits and sunglasses even.

"Okay, that sounds great. Where are you going to get the bandannas from?"

"I can make them. I have a sewing machine. I'll buy several yards of material and get sewing. I make them all the time for Red."

Drake sat back in the chair in his small living room and listened to her talk about how she planned to visit the fabric store and pick out dog-appropriate designs. She loved animals, old people, living on the beach, she could sew, and she could write romance novels. *Wonder if she can cook?*

"That sounds great, Ruby. By the way, are you free for dinner sometime?"

CHAPTER 5

*H*er gaze darted around the room. She jumped up from her chair and palmed her chest. Was he asking her out on a date?

"You mean to discuss the plans to save Shady Grove, right?" She drew in her bottom lip and held it with her teeth.

"That too. But if you're not seeing anyone, I'd like to have dinner with you sometime."

She had to think this over. He just broke up with his girlfriend, and he was already rebounding? That seemed a bit strange. Maybe he was afraid of commitment. Oh great. Then perhaps he wouldn't even follow through with the golf tournament. She had to keep him focused. He sounded like a guy who threw in the towel too quickly. But what was it Grandmother said…Nothing ventured nothing gained.

"Dinner sounds great. I'll bring all my notes about the upcoming events. You bring yours about the golf tournament."

"Okay, where do you want to have dinner?"

The silence was thick enough to cut with a knife. After a long pause, she found the words to reply. "Here. Come over here. I'll make dinner for us."

It took her all of twenty minutes to spruce up her cottage. It was a beautiful evening, so she set the table outside for their dinner. She used her turquoise woven placemats with her white dinnerware, and in the center of the table, she placed a milk white vase with a bouquet of summer annuals in yellow, purple, and white she'd purchased at the market.

The sun was just beginning to set. A few people held hands as they walked along the wet, packed sand, making Ruby envious of the lovebirds. A timer went off in the kitchen, sending her rushing in. The smell of pork chops wafted through the tiny place, causing her tummy to grumble in anticipation of the taste. She hoped it was as good as it smelled. She set the dish on a trivet to cool. She removed the chopped salad from the fridge and sliced the bread, stealing a small piece to suppress her hunger pangs. She pulled off the paper covering of the brand-new bottle of salad dressing and gave it a shake. She dropped her eyelids as blinding headlights shot through her window. It was him. She quickly dried her hands on the apron, slipping it over her head and tossing it on the hook on the wall. She fluffed her hair with her fingers, tucking it behind her ears and made it to the door when he knocked.

Gleaming, toothy smiles crossed their faces at once. They both laughed at the same time, compelling them to laugh even harder.

"Please," she said, motioning, "come in."

He produced a bottle of wine he'd held behind him. "For dinner," he said, grinning ear to ear.

She gingerly took the bottle and placed it on the counter.

"Something smells so wonderful."

"Thanks. I hope you like pork chops." She began to rummage around for a wine bottle opener. She found it, holding it out to him to do the honors.

He ripped the paper off the bottle and had it open in no time flat. He was an expert, she determined.

"Glasses?" He looked around the small kitchen.

"Up there," she said, tipping her chin as she placed the chops on the plates.

He removed two stemless wineglasses and filled them. "What can I do to help?"

"If you can grab the basket of bread, I'll bring out the salad."

He did as she asked. She scrutinized his moves as he made long, slow strides out the screen door. A bolt of excitement flashed through her when he suddenly turned around and caught her staring. He winked at her while he used his back to open the door, holding it open for her to come through. Her face now hot, she could only imagine how red it was. She walked through the doorway and placed the large bowl of greens on the table, took the dressing she had wedged under her arm and placed it next to the bowl. When he set the basket of bread down, their hands brushed, and a thrill rushed through her veins she'd not felt in a long time.

"Have a seat. I'll grab the plates with the chops." She hurried inside, trying to run from the awkward moment.

She held the rim of the sink and counted to ten. "Ruby Bennett. This is just dinner." She grabbed the two plates, and while slowly breathing in and out, made her way outside.

"You have such a neat setup here," he said, nodding toward the ocean.

"I know. I have to pinch myself constantly. It's a dream come true." She helped herself to the salad.

The white lights that hung around the covered porch and the candles that she'd strategically placed on the railings of the porch gave off enough allure to set the scene of a romantic dinner. Was that her intention?

"How's the pork chop?" she asked, trying to keep the dinner conversation moving.

"Tender and juicy."

Her gaze dropped to his hands and arms. It had been a while since she admired such raw man beauty. Suddenly, he glanced up from his plate.

A throaty noise escaped her lips. "I was just admiring your tan."

He rolled his arm and looked it over. "I get a fair amount of sun."

"I probably get too much. I can hear Grandmother now. 'Make sure you put on plenty of sunscreen!'" She giggled.

After dinner, they walked on the beach. Red ran up ahead, keeping them in sight. They laughed about his silly antics. The sun had set, and the moon was out, lighting up the sky. The lights from the houses along the beach lit up the rest of the sand. A small group of people had a bonfire going, and from the looks of it, couples were cuddling and kissing, and some were roasting marshmallows.

"We didn't talk about the fund-raisers," Drake said, his voice low and sultry, sending a wave of shivers up Ruby's spine.

"I know. We talked about everything else."

They had too. He told her about how he'd put himself through law school. It was important for people to know that he wasn't some spoiled rich kid who got everything handed to him. He worked for it. And he worked hard. She admired that about him. She opened up to him about how her parents had died in a car crash when she was in college. How after graduation she came for a visit at the cottage to see her grandmother and how she never left. She told him how she had been in a low place in her life when she adopted Red, and how he made her feel whole and happy again.

"A dog did that for you, huh? Maybe I should get one. I might have better luck with a dog than I've had with girl-friends." He playfully knocked shoulders with her.

Pulling her head back, a deep belly laugh roared. "Dogs can do a very special thing that not even humans can do for each other."

"Well is that so," he teased.

They walked almost to the end of the beach when they both stopped and faced each other. He dug his hands into his pockets and rolled back on his heels. "I know we just met and all, but I've really enjoyed my evening with you, Ruby."

"I had a nice time too. I think the common bond we share with wanting to save Shady Grove Place is what makes it so special." She batted her lashes a couple of times.

"It's not exactly my desire to save Shady Grove Place. That's your desire. I'm just attempting to hold up my end of the deal."

"Wait. I know that's how this started, but I thought you were really into doing this. Because it's so important to your dad. Not just to me. It's not some kind of fleeting gesture of kindness, or trying to date a girl kind of thing." She turned away and started walking back toward the cottage.

He placed a hand on her shoulder. "Hold on a minute. Don't walk away."

She stopped, but she didn't turn to face him.

He moved around her and tipped her chin up with his finger.

She pushed it away, crossing her arms in defiance.

"I didn't mean it like that. You know I'm helping you because of my dad. Why else would I do it?"

"I don't know. Maybe to try to get me to go out with you?"

"Well that thought did cross my mind, but…" He leaned in closer.

A momentary tug of emotion squeezed at her chest.

He leaned in and cupped her face, pulling her close. Their mouths touched softly, then he stepped back.

"Don't tell me you don't feel something too."

She could feel the intensity of his stare, and it made her pick up her feet and start walking. Fast.

"Ruby. Wait."

She picked up the pace and soon was jogging. She made it to the porch quickly. She could hear him breathing heavily as he came up behind her.

He bent over holding his knees, trying to catch his breath. When he rose, he palmed his chest. "I'm sorry if I said or did something wrong. I just thought we had a connection. And by the way, Red has for sure gotten you in shape. I might need to consider getting a dog." He reached over and grabbed the water glass off the table and gulped it.

"Yeah, he loves to fetch and play Frisbee. We run quite a bit."

"Listen, about the kiss. It wasn't anything big."

She pursed her lips. "I figured as much. Listen, why don't we go over the details later. I'm kind of tired."

"Can you at least share with me what Mr. Jensen said about perhaps paying some of the tax debt off."

"Oh, that. Yes, he said he could pay five thousand toward it. But he'll only do it if we have the rest. Otherwise, he'll need it for attorney fees for filing bankruptcy."

"The way I calculate it, we can raise about six thousand dollars from the golf tournament. If Mr. Jensen tosses in five thousand, we only need one thousand dollars from the book and bake sale. Maybe we don't need the other fund-raisers."

"We still need money to fix the place up. There's furniture to replace, cracking sidewalks to repair, a swimming pool that needs resurfacing and the list goes on and on."

He stepped closer toward her. "Can we start over, please?"

She nodded.

"I do like you, Ruby Bennett. I know why my dad is so fond of you. You're spunky, cute, and you have a big heart."

She blinked at him, her smile slipping around the edges. "Thank you. I can see the family resemblance. I bet your dad was one foxy man in his heyday."

He puffed out his chest. "Yeah, they say the apple doesn't fall far from the tree."

"I hope you'll see what we are doing is so fulfilling in so many ways. One of these days we're going to be old. Don't you want someone to care about us?"

"Of course, I do. That's what kids are for, right?" He belted a hearty laugh.

"Dessert?" She elevated her eyebrows.

A sigh danced on his lips. "And she can cook!"

"What is that supposed to mean?" She tilted her head.

"Oh nothing. Inside joke."

CHAPTER 6

Drake beamed all the way home. Something about her made him giddy. Was that even possible for men to feel that emotion? Maybe not giddy. But hopeful. Yeah. That's a better word for the way he was feeling. He punched the accelerator and drove like a madman down the freeway while the radio blared.

He turned the door and opened it wide, stepping into his apartment. He tossed his keys, wallet and cell phone onto the small entry table and entered the dimly lit living room. He lowered himself onto the black leather sofa, leaning his head back onto the forgiving cushion and closed his eyelids. Ruby's smiling face popped right into his mind. A slow grin crossed his lips.

He didn't believe in jumping out of one frying pan into another, but this was different. Wasn't it? She just happened to come into his life by mere circumstance. Chrissy wasn't really the girl for him anyway. Now that he thought about it, she was a bit superficial, and if he had to see her eat one more salad, it wouldn't be too soon for him. And in a way, he got his wish.

At that moment, his cell chimed, letting him know he had an incoming call. He pulled himself out of the comfy sofa and retrieved his phone. It was Ruby. He'd already put her in his contacts.

"Hey, did I forget something?"

She giggled into the phone. "No. I just wanted to tell you again how happy I am that we are working on this project together."

He crossed back to the living room and sat . "I'm happy that we are working on it together too." He grimaced after he realized he'd almost said word for word what she'd said. "I hope it all goes well for Shady Grove Place," he added.

"I'm happy how the town is rallying with the donations. The bakery is providing cookies and cupcakes, the volunteer fire department is going to pass the boot at the bridge to passing cars and see if they can get some change to give to us, and the library in Sandy Cove is donating several used books to our book sale. I just think it's fantastic how everyone is coming out and showing their support," she said.

"I agree. I'm excited about the golf tournament. It's a week from tomorrow. I'm sure some of those guys will round up their donation."

"Okay, so keep me posted on how that goes. I've got a few loose ends to tie up for the book and bake sale two weeks from tomorrow. You're going to come for that, right?"

"I wouldn't miss it."

"Ahh. That's so sweet of you to say," she said.

"Well, if I missed it, I'd miss seeing you."

A long pause pulled at his heartstrings as he waited for her reply.

"I can't wait to see you too."

He blew out a big breath. "I wasn't sure how that was going to play out. Glad you didn't make me feel stupid."

"You don't know me very well, but I feel like I'm a good judge of character. I like you. I don't say that often, but you have empathy which I need in my friends, and you're pretty cute too."

He tossed his head back deeper into the cushion, a low belly laugh roaring up from deep within. "Cute?"

"Uh-huh."

"I was going to tell you the same thing."

"Oh?"

"I like the way you smile, showing off that little dimple just to the right of your mouth. Or the way your eyes dance, and your sweet giggle. Yeah, you're cute." He cautiously paused.

"We're also thirty-something. Do thirty-year-old people identify each other as cute?"

"Probably not. I was going to say sexy, but we don't know each other like that, yet."

"Yet?" Ruby's voice rose an octave.

"I hope after all the events are over with, you'll still want to see me. Or am I being too presumptuous?" Drake poked his lips out, wondering if he just asked another stupid question.

"Let's don't get ahead of ourselves. One day at a time is my motto. Listen gotta run, but I did want to thank you, and please let me know how the tournament goes."

"Okay. Talk to you later, Ruby."

He tossed the phone onto the end table and crossed his arms. That was one weird conversation. It started out like some high school banter turned sexy tease, finishing with a businesslike tone. He shook his head, then shrugged. Dating. Relationships. Maybe they were not meant for him after all.

RUBY STOOD at the window and looked out. She could see and hear the waves as they came crashing onto shore. Sexy, huh? She thought he was kind of sexy too. She hugged her arms tighter. Ruby laughed loudly, trying to shake off the strong signals this good-looking man was sending via telephone lines or was it just her imagination?

AFTER THEIR MORNING ritual of walking the beach and searching for seashells, Ruby and Red made a trip over to Shady Grove Place. Mrs. Parker was sitting in one of the chairs in the main living area, chatting with one of the residents. She smiled at Ruby and waved.

Red trotted ahead of Ruby and made a beeline to the residents for his dose of love. He yawned, then plopped down at the feet of one of the residents as they rubbed his head.

"How are things going with the event planning, Ruby?" Old Mr. Jarvis asked.

"Going well. The golf tournament is a week from today. Then two weeks from today we'll have the book and bake sale."

"I could get out my golf clubs and join the group," Mr. Jarvis said.

Ruby's jaw released. In her peripheral view, she could see Mrs. Parker shaking her head vehemently.

"Well that's very nice of you to offer, Mr. Jarvis, but I think they have a full group already signed up. But if you'd like to help me with the book and bake sale, that would be most helpful." She patted him on the shoulder.

Suddenly the door opened, and in walked Mr. Jensen. Both Ruby and Mrs. Parker gave each other a strange look, then met him over at the reception counter.

"What brings you in here today?" Mrs. Parker asked.

"Hazel, this is my business. Don't you think I can stop in anytime I want?" He looked at her over the top of his glasses. He lowered his head and began searching the desktop.

"Is there something in particular you are looking for?" Mrs. Parker piqued her brows almost to her hairline.

"A letter from the city. Did one come today or yesterday?"

Mrs. Parker joined Mr. Jensen on the other side of the counter. "You mean this?" She held out a white business-size envelope.

He abruptly took it out of her hand and stared at it. "Yep, that's it."

"What is it, Mr. Jensen?" Ruby asked, concern surely written all over her face.

"I went down to city hall to see about getting an extension on the taxes due. This here shows they granted us an extra thirty days." He waved the letter around in the air.

"That's fantastic, Mr. Jensen. With thirty more days, I'm almost positive we can save Shady Grove Place!" Ruby's voice rang with optimism.

"Let's hope so, Ruby. This is all the time we're going to get. I have some other news to share." He leaned his elbows on the counter.

Ruby stepped in closer.

Mrs. Parker moved closer toward Mr. Jensen.

Now that he had their undivided attention, he spoke, his voice steady and calm.

"I had a fella reach out to me about fixing the swimming pool. For free."

Mrs. Parker squealed.

"Don't go saying anything just yet. But he's coming by later today to get a better look at it. His dad used to live here. He's passed away, but when he heard what we were striving to do, he called me."

"How'd he hear about what we're doing?" Mrs. Parker asked.

Mr. Jensen tipped his head toward Ruby. "Saw some flyers this young lady is passing out."

Ruby rocked back on her heels. "I'm trying to get the word out."

"You're doing a fine job too. I appreciate everything you're doing for this place."

AFTER THAT BIT of good news, Ruby was floating on cloud nine. An extension for the taxes due, a guy willing to fix the swimming pool for free—wait! That gave her another idea. Maybe she could find more people willing to donate their time and skill to fix the place up. She did some searching on the internet for charities that might be able to help, and when she found a few possible organizations, she picked up her phone and reached out to them.

It was a little disheartening at first, but she totally understood their reluctance in helping to fix up Shady Grove Place. After all, it was owned by a businessman who'd let it fall apart. Why should anyone donate their labor, skills, and supplies to someone who didn't see the importance of it in the first place?

But when she reached out to a church organization, she got a completely different answer. Not only were they able, but they were willing. And for the second time that day, Ruby Bennett got good news.

She called Mr. Jensen and shared the information.

"I reached out to a neighboring church that advertised they participated in local outreach to seniors. It was a shot in the dark, but I made a call, and they are very happy about helping Shady Grove Place. They have several parishioners who have construction skills. They said if we get the paint and supplies, they can furnish the labor."

"Okay. So maybe with the fund-raiser, we can purchase some paint and things," Mr. Jensen replied.

"I think it means we need another fund-raiser too. I think I'll put into motion my walk a dog on the beach campaign."

"Walk a dog on the beach?" Mr. Jensen replied with skepticism.

"I'm going to make bandannas and sell them for the event. I'll contact one or two food trucks, and we'll have a relay race with dogs. It'll be something fun for the entire family."

Mr. Jensen laughed. "Okay, go for it. Isn't that what young people say nowadays?"

Ruby giggled. "Yes, although that sort of went out a few years ago. But no worries, I gotcha covered."

After she got off the phone with him, she went to work on the beach event. She contacted two food truck companies and set that up. Then she drove to the fabric store and bought twenty yards of fabric in varying patterns. Some had dog bones on them, some had happy dog faces, some were just with designs, like plaid and shapes. And she even found a few solids that would work.

After she got home, she made a call to Drake. It went to voice mail.

"Hey, it's me," she said after the beep. "I have something great to tell you. Why don't you come over tonight? I'll toss a large salad, throw some burgers on the grill, and make a pitcher of margaritas," she said, putting her little spin of a Spanish accent on margarita. "Call me." Click.

WHEN DRAKE WAS able to check his messages, his pulse raced when he heard her voice. His big smile quickly faded when he heard salad. It didn't really matter; he just wanted to see her.

CHAPTER 7

She double-checked herself in the long mirror mounted behind her bedroom door. She tugged at the hems of her shorts. She turned slightly and looked at her backside. The shorts were short, but it was summer. The turquoise blue tank top made the color of her eyes pop. She pulled her hair back into a ponytail and secured it with a turquoise rubber band. She brushed on some peach-colored blush and rolled on some lip gloss in a color that coordinated with the blush and spritzed on some cologne, finally slipping her feet into some black and turquoise flip-flops.

In the kitchen, she tossed the salad, adding bacon bits, shredded cheese, cherry tomatoes, and croutons. She took the ground beef and added her secret weapon to tasty burgers and shaped them into patties. She sliced cheddar cheese to top them with after grilling and went to work slicing onion, spooning out pickles from the jar, and layering lettuce leaves on the plate for garnishing the burgers. Satisfied everything was underway, she made up the margaritas. And just for good measure, dumped an extra shot full of tequila in the blend.

Now all she needed was Drake.

After a short time, he rapped on the door, sending Red running and barking.

"Calm down, Red. It's just Drake," Ruby said, trailing after the long-legged, tail-wagging companion.

The temperatures during the day were heating up just a bit, so the air conditioning was on in the little cottage. She opened the door, then popped open the screen door.

"Wow. You look very summery and cute," he said, stepping inside.

"Summery and cute. Now I get two words to describe me."

"It's the colors. The white shorts and blue top say hot."

She could feel her cheeks blush. She tucked a stray hair behind her ear and tilted her head slightly. "Hot?"

"I upped my vocabulary from cute." He winked, setting her heart pounding.

"Follow me." She motioned him to join her in the kitchen.

"I don't know what you like in your salad, so I call this the kitchen sink salad." She held out the large blue bowl filled with greens and cherry tomatoes.

He pursed his lips.

"What? Don't you like salad?"

"Well, let's just say, I've seen enough salad to last a while. Chrissy. My ex. that's all she ever ate. I got so tired of seeing her munch on greens like a rabbit. But I'm sure your salad will be delicious."

She opened the refrigerator door and stuck her head inside. She began to pull out some containers. "No, if you don't like salad, I would rather serve you something you'd like. Potato salad?"

He nodded.

"Fruit salad?"

He flashed her a wide grin.

"You're in luck. I just so happen to have a little left over from the other day. It's enough to share." She pulled her head to the right and motioned him to follow. She led him outside to the gas grill. "How are your grilling skills?" She lifted the black cover and ignited the flame. Then she grabbed a scraping tool and began to clean off the grill.

"Fair," he said, taking the tool from her.

"Good. I'll grab the patties."

She took off like a rocket and soon returned with the platter of four large perfectly round hamburger patties. She tossed them on the grill and stood back while they sizzled, and soon the smells of grilled beef wafted through the air.

The outside temperature had dropped considerably, thankfully, from the ocean breeze that blew through and made living on the coast so wonderful even in the heat of the summer. They set the outside table for dinner.

"These burgers are great. I can't quite put my finger on what I'm tasting. Onion, spices?" He cocked his head.

"My secret spice. If I told you, I'd have to kill you." She smirked.

"Oh, well, by all means then. Keep your secret." He laughed.

"No, it's onion soup mix. It makes them moist, flavorful, and people just love them. And, you don't really need any additional spices. Sometimes I sprinkle pepper too." She took a bite of her fruit salad. "I'm glad you aren't a fan of tossed salads. I love fruit too." She inserted the fork into her mouth all the while drinking in his broad shoulders and dimple. Dimple! He had one almost in the same spot as she. Why didn't she notice that before? She swallowed, pointing to his face. "Dimple. You have one too. In the exact same place as I have one." Her eyes grew large as her voice climbed in octave.

He chuckled. "Yes, I do." He hung his head.

"Why are you embarrassed by it?"

"I don't know," he said, blushing.

"Well, I think it's cu—"

"Cute?" He finished her sentence for her.

"Charming. Sexy." Her husky tone scared her. Where the heck did that come from?

"Sexy, huh?" His gaze bore a hole right through her, and she squirmed in her seat.

"You're sexy, I'm sexy, sounds like a lot of sexiness going on here at the table." He put his fork down and reached his hand across the table.

Ruby hesitated for a second, slowly sliding her hand across and into his grasp. The warmth of his hand sent shivers down her spine, and her tummy tightened some.

"Thank you for asking me over for dinner. You mentioned you had some good news." He lifted their clutched hands and pressed a kiss to her hand.

She flinched, then drew in her bottom lip, holding it securely in place with her teeth. Then she released the hold and straightened her back. Trying to keep her voice steady and unnerved she said, "Yes, Mr. Jensen came by Shady Grove Place with some good news. Someone is going to resurface the swimming pool for free." She pulled her hand back and picked up her glass of margarita. "And I made a few calls today, and I have some folks lined up to help with painting and outside repair. I also contacted a church, and they are going to offer some skilled labor to help spruce things up." She drew a taste of the lime drink, followed by another.

"Wow. Well done, Ruby. This just might work."

"I hope so. Because the only way Mr. Jensen will be able to sustain the place is if we get back to full occupancy, once the renovations are done. He can then start reaping the rent and keep things going. It's really a nice place. So many loved living there over the years." She forked a piece of watermelon.

"I like the way you think." He slid his chair out and stood.

Ruby did the same, taking her margarita with her.

"Walk on the beach?" He held out his arm.

"Sounds lovely." She took his arm, and they strolled on wet sand while Red played his usual game of running up and past them, making a quick turn and racing full speed ahead of them.

"I never had a pet before. I think I'm missing out on something." He took his free hand and placed it on hers as she held his arm.

"I don't know what I'd do without Red. He's my sounding board when I'm angry, he's my shrink when I'm sad, and he's my funny little man when I'm feeling silly."

"I can tell he's a great companion to you." He squeezed her arm against his body.

She immediately took notice of his firm frame. As they walked, she bumped into his hip. She profusely excused herself laughing it off as an accident. *This guy doesn't have an ounce of fat on him. He is all bones, muscles, and taut flesh.* Her heart raced, making her feel jittery. Or was it the margarita?

"We should be getting back. I need to put the food away," she said, grimacing at the lame excuse to get away from the tortuous pull he had on her.

He slowed to a stop, then whirled her around to face him. Slipping his hand to her waist, he pulled her toward him. She held her breath and braced herself for the kiss. He leaned down and placed a soft kiss on her lips. She closed her eyes, moving her hands up and around his neck, holding him in place. He pressed her lips firmer, opening up her mouth some, quickening her pulse and raising the heat level from blushing to hot. She let out a soft groan.

He held her back and stared into her eyes. "This is really nice," he said, rocking her in his arms.

She nodded, finding it difficult to speak. He took her voice away as well as her breath.

He turned her around, slipping his arm over her shoulder as they walked slowly back to the cottage. "I hope you don't mind that I kissed you. You just looked so beautiful, and I was overcome by it and reacted."

"Don't apologize. I'm glad you did." She snuggled into his embrace.

"I know I just came out of a relationship. I don't want you to think I do this a lot. She dumped me."

"I see. Well, I don't date much anyway. I write romance, but unfortunately, I don't get to enjoy it in real life, much." She raised her head and gazed up at him.

He lowered his head and kissed her.

When they got to the cottage, Red was lying on the porch waiting for them.

After they put the food away and cleaned up the kitchen, they sat at the table and talked.

"You know my dad talked about you a lot. I never even gave you a second thought. My bad," he said, taking her hand in his.

She swirled her thumb along his and smiled. "He talked about you a lot, too, and I never gave you a thought either." She shrugged.

"I guess we have Dad to thank for getting us together. He'll be happy to hear it." He pulled her hand up to his mouth and pressed a kiss.

"I guess so." A girly giggle escaped her lips.

"So, where do we go from here?"

The way he looked at her set her right on fire. Her stomach pitched and rolled, her pulse quickened, and her mouth was completely dry. She wetted her lips. "We take each day as it comes, Drake. I'm not going anywhere. I don't want to rush anything. The kisses are sweet, and I don't want you to think I don't like them. I do. But let's get the organizing done for the events and reevaluate our relationship after that."

He frowned at her, causing him to release her hands from his hold.

"What's wrong?" she asked.

"I just thought we had something. Remember you invited me over here."

"Yes, yes I did. I enjoy your company. I wanted to share the good news with you."

"What about the kisses?" He began to walk toward the front door.

"Drake. Don't go. I loved the kisses. But I don't want to lose sight of what it is we're doing."

"Lose sight of what we are doing? Clearly, it isn't forming a relationship as boyfriend and girlfriend. It's more about golf tournaments, book and bake sales." He placed a hand on the doorknob and turned it. "No worries. I'll get your donations. I'll do whatever is required to get Shady Grove Place up and running. But I'll still be moving my dad out." He opened the door and rushed out, slamming it behind him.

Tears rolled down her face quickly, and soon she was sobbing in her hands.

CHAPTER 8

He sat in his car for a few moments, trying to catch his breath and steady the anger he felt brewing. How could he be so dumb as to fall for the oldest trick in the book. She wasn't looking for a boyfriend. She just wanted to use him for whatever he could do to bring Shady Grove Place back from the dead. He fired up the car engine and drove home.

Over the next few days, he ignored her phone calls. She didn't leave any messages, so that was easy enough. Nothing to return. When Saturday came, and it was time to participate in the tournament, he had a difficult time concentrating on the game. All he could think about was her. It drove him mad. He wanted her, but he didn't. He had pride.

"Drake, where's your head at buddy?"

Drake shrugged, then hung his head low.

"Is it your dad?"

"No." He walked toward the ball cart.

"If you keep playing this well, we should come in before dark and in very last place."

"It's just a game, Skip. Besides, it's for charity."

"Yes, I know, but what's got you down? You were so excited about this."

He climbed into the driver's seat and waited for Skip to get in.

"It's over a girl, isn't it?" Skip leaned back and chuckled.

"It always is," Drake replied.

"Yeah, we love them, and they make us crazy at the same time," Skip said, shaking his head.

"The thing is, Skip, I just met her. How can I feel like this when I just met the darn girl?"

"Fate?" Skip hunched his shoulders, then reached over and patted Drake on the shoulder. "Tell her how you feel."

RUBY AND RED got ready for a visit to Shady Grove Place. She filled the back seat with as many boxes as she could and drove over to the place. She carried one box and gave Red a command to come. Juggling the heavy box, she managed to open the door, grabbing the bottom corner of it with her foot before it closed. Red squeezed through the small opening. Ruby blew her bangs back that drooped past her forehead. Using her foot again, she heaved the door open. While the door flew open, she ran in, just in time for the door to close. She made a mental note that the door should be more user-friendly.

"Do you have a dolly I can borrow?" Ruby called out as she struggled with the oversized box, her hair falling into her face still.

Mrs. Parker came scurrying out from the counter. "Yes, let me get it." She took off down the hall.

Ruby sat the box in a corner and waited. Soon Mrs. Parker came around the corner, pushing an old and rusty dolly that had seen better days. Ruby smirked. "Well, it will have to do." She took the squeaky appliance and rolled it toward the door.

"I'll open up apartment six, and you can store these boxes inside it," Mrs. Parker called out.

The dolly made the rest of the job easy for Ruby. She loaded that thing right up to the top and rolled it into apartment six as Mrs. Parker had requested.

"Have you heard how Drake did with the golf tournament?" Mrs. Parker handed her a cup of cold water from the dispenser.

Ruby shook her head. "Not a word."

Mrs. Parker wrinkled up her face. "Are you two on the outs?"

Ruby's face gave it away.

"You are!"

"It was just a misunderstanding. It'll blow over," Ruby said, not really believing it would.

"What happened?" Mrs. Parker asked.

Ruby giggled. She put nosey and parker together and recalled her grandmother using that description about other nosey people.

"It's a long story, Mrs. Parker. Don't worry about it. The book and bake sale will go on as planned, and I've been busy making doggy bandannas to sell. They're coming out so cute. I have fabric with dogs in spacesuits, wiener dogs with sweaters, and one of my favorites, paw prints in purple. I might just have to make one for Red." She was sure her bright smile lit up the room when she spoke Red's name.

At that moment, the two ladies turned their heads toward the sounds of the front door opening. There stood Drake, still in his golf attire.

Mrs. Parker and Ruby exchanged looks, then Mrs. Parker took off like a comet and rushed around the counter, busying herself with who knows what.

"Hey," Ruby managed to squeak out despite the pounding in her chest.

"Hey," he said, moving away from the door and closer toward her.

All that did was make her heart pound even harder if that were possible.

"How was the golf game?" She tipped her chin upward and motioned toward his golf shorts and collared polo shirt. Even she knew golfers wore that when out on the course.

"It was good." He held out an envelope.

She gingerly took it, turning it over and studying the flap. It wasn't sealed. She lifted it and took out the piece of paper. It was a check made out to Mr. Jensen in the amount of ten thousand dollars. She tore her eyes from the dollar sign and gazed at him.

"This is way more than what you thought." She tilted her head, shaking it slightly.

"Yes, some of the guys threw in extra." He turned around.

"Wait. Drake."

He stopped.

She moved slowly toward him, then moved around him to face him. "Listen, about the other night." She grimaced. *Why do apologies always start like that?* She swallowed hard. "I'm sorry that we got off to a bad start."

He didn't blink an eyelash. "I didn't think we got off to a bad start. It ended badly." He crossed his arms and stepped back.

His uneasiness about being close to her resonated deeply with her. *What about the kiss?* "Okay, ended badly. Where can we go from here?" She held back the tears that tried to escape by willing each and every one of them away. She refused to let him see her emotional. She was too strong for that.

"I don't really know, Ruby."

His few words left her speechless. How was she to move forward if he wouldn't engage her?

"Can we start over?"

"Is that what you want? And how do I know it's sincere?" He uncrossed his arms and let them dangle at his side, then inserted his hands into his pockets.

She sensed his feeling awkward about the situation and attempted to help him feel at ease.

"Drake, I was always sincere. I don't know why you jumped off the deep end thinking anything else."

"Oh, really? How come when I tried to get close, you backed off? All you wanted to discuss were the details of the events planned to save Shady Grove Place."

"I don't know. Maybe because I was scared? We'd just met, we already shared a kiss. I just felt it was moving a bit fast for me." She lowered her head and stared at her painted-pink toenails. *A few are chipped. I need a pedicure.* She raised her gaze and studied his face. "I like you a lot. Heck, even Red likes you. That's saying a lot. He's a great judge of character." She let out a tiny laugh, then quickly became serious once again. "Come on. Let bygones be bygones." *Yikes. Another Grandmother saying.* "Please?" She held out her hands to him.

Drake pulled his hands out of his pockets.

She stepped nearer, still holding her hands open for him.

He moved a little closer, then laced his fingers with her.

"Now that wasn't so bad, was it?" A smile curled up at the corners of her mouth.

"Torture," he said, then winked at her. He gripped her hands firmly; shivers ignited up her spine.

"Torture?" she asked.

"I've thought about you so much and what I wanted to say to you."

"Then why didn't you pick up when I called?" Suspicion rang in her voice.

He shrugged. "Not ready to wear my heart out on my sleeve I guess."

"I like that about you, Drake. You're sensitive and caring. Don't be ashamed or apologize for that. It's a great characteristic to have."

"I like you, Ruby Bennett. I like you a lot." His stare made her blush.

"I like you, too, Drake Carrolton."

"Okay, so what can I do to do help with the book sale?"

She nodded toward the door. "I have some boxes in my car."

He grabbed the dolly and made his way toward the door. Ruby looked back over to Mrs. Parker and smiled.

Mrs. Parker mouthed, *See I told you.*

Ruby lifted her shoulders to her ears and beamed. Then she ran ahead to open the door for Drake.

"By the way, this door isn't very user-friendly," she said as they made their way outside.

"I'll put it on the list," he answered.

CHAPTER 9

She kept busy ironing out the last details for the book and bake sale. Things seemed to be in order, and they were just waiting for the day. Boxes of books from her author friends took up most of the space in her small living room. In the evening, in between writing, she made a few doggy bandannas, having Red be the model.

"Oh my. That is so cute, Red," Ruby said, watching him prance around with his dogs in spacesuits one.

She kept the triangle pieces of fabric in a large, clear container. Since they were cut out, it was just a matter of stitching the hems. She had about a dozen more to make then she'd be done. She took a break and poured herself a glass of water and went outside.

In the distance, a summer rainstorm was brewing. An occasional lightning bolt lit up the dark sky. It was a pleasant night, and people and dogs were still walking the shoreline, getting in a last walk before the rain came. Ruby had lived on the little island long enough that she could determine how long before the rain made its way to her. She still had a couple of hours according to the distance of the lightning. She took the few steps down, wiggling her toes through the warm sand.

Red came out onto the porch, stretching his lean body and yawning. Ruby giggled. "No, boy, we're not going for a walk. I just came outside to take in a deep breath of the sea air." A big breeze shot through, blowing her hair in every direction. "Oh, this is going to be a nice storm." She turned and went back inside to batten down the hatches. Sometimes the thunderstorms could be intense. But the next day, blue skies. It was all worth it to Ruby.

As she cleaned up the living room and put away her sewing machine, the rain began to gently fall on her roof. At first, it was just a soft whisper, then came the pounding. Soon her lights flickered, and the wind blew open the screen door. She ran to the door, trying to reel it back in. Feeling the strength of the gusts, she held tight. She finally managed to get it free from the wind's clutches, locking it with the eye and hook closure. She could see in the distance the waves really churning. A doozy of a storm for sure. She shut the main door and finished getting the house ready so she could go to bed.

She'd just snuggled under the covers with her Kindle when her phone chimed. She smiled when she saw who was calling.

"Hey there," she said.

"I just saw on the weather report a storm coming your way," Drake said with concern.

"Yep. It's going to be a big one. I've already battened down the hatches. We're good."

"As long as I've lived in Florida, I always still get spooked over these storms," Drake said.

"Naw. I've been through hurricanes and came out unscathed. A little thunder and lightning don't scare me. However, Red doesn't like it too much." Ruby petted Red as he lay next to her.

"Well, be careful," Drake said.

"Of course. Hey, Drake?"

"Yes?"

"Would you like to come over for dinner tomorrow?"

"Why don't you let me take you out instead? You've been doing so much for Shady Grove Place. Take a break and let someone else do the cooking."

She rested into her pillow. She hadn't been out to a restaurant in months. In fact, maybe the last time was with her boyfriend. She usually just made her meals or grabbed a bite at the few local places like the fish truck, or the café just before you crossed the bridge. Sometimes she'd really treat herself, and when she went into the town ten miles away to do her shopping, she'd stop at the eateries there. It was more of the same. A taco shack that served great fish tacos, a fast-food drive-in place, and a café that had the best shrimp and grits she'd ever had. Just a little hole in the wall too.

"Dinner sounds nice," she said.

"Okay, great. Let's see, Orlando is too far for dinner. What if I meet you at this neat café that is about ten miles from you? It has the best shrimp and grits I've ever tasted."

She leaned forward with the phone glued to her ear still. "Polly's?"

"Yes, that's the place. I guess I should have known you've been there before," he said.

"I didn't realize you'd ever been."

"Oh, I take Dad there quite a bit. He loves that place."

"Why don't you pick up your dad and we can go together? I know he'd love to get out of Shady Grove Place for a ride."

"I guess. I just thought it would be nice just the two of us," Drake said, a tone of defeat in his voice.

Ruby thought fast. "Oh, that's a lovely gesture, Drake. How about we take your dad to dinner with us and after we drop him back by his place you come in for a nightcap and dessert?"

"Dessert and a nightcap?"

His words came out low and sexy, and it raised the hair on her arms. Did he do that on purpose?

"Ahh. I hear chocolate and red wine go together rather well," she said.

"Sounds great. I'll call Dad and let him know, and we'll see you around six tomorrow night."

"Okay, Drake. Perfect. Looking forward to seeing you. Good night."

"Good night, Ruby."

She tossed the phone on the nightstand. Closing her eyes, she recalled her wise grandmother's sayings. *What was it that Grandmother used to say? When you least expect it.* She picked up her Kindle and tried to read a few paragraphs. But it was no use. She closed it, placing it next to her phone, and crawled out of bed. "Hot chocolate. Maybe that would help," she said aloud as she padded toward the kitchen.

"Okay, Red. What do you think?" She turned around, showing off what she picked to wear to dinner.

Red blinked.

"Yeah, not really your thing, right? You're more of a bandanna sort of fella." She laughed.

She took a long look at herself in the mirror. A sundress seemed like the perfect thing to wear to dinner. And the pink-and-white spaghetti strap V-neck dress looked and felt good. She slipped her feet into white sandals, finishing with her hair and makeup. She didn't like to wear heavy makeup, so a light foundation with sunscreen, a little mascara, and some lip gloss gave her the look she liked. She decided to wear her hair down and hoped she wouldn't regret it. It had been an unusually warm and muggy day on the coast.

Red barked as he pawed at the front door.

"Drake and Joel are here," she said.

She went to the door and opened it. There stood both Drake and his dad, Joel.

"I hope you don't mind. Dad wanted to see your place." Drake pulled his shoulders up and let them fall.

"Not at all," she said, opening the door wide. Drake had his dad's arm and helped him inside.

"Hi, Ruby," Joel said as he shuffled inside.

"Good evening, Joel. No walker tonight?" She looked up at Drake.

"Oh, that thing is such a monstrosity. Who wants to be with an old man who has to use a walker?" he grunted, then smiled when Red came up and licked his hand.

"Besides, it doesn't roll well in the sand." He glanced up and grinned.

"True. I didn't think about that," Ruby said, taking his other arm. "Do you want to see the rest of the place?"

She took him through the small cottage. He made comments showing how much he liked it. When they were through with the tour, he made a disclosure.

"See. This is what I need. A little cottage on the beach."

Drake shot a look to Ruby, then chuckled.

"No, Dad. You don't. What you need is your nice efficiency apartment at Shady Grove Place where you're among friends."

He waved off the notion. "I do like it there, but I liked it better back in the day."

"We're trying to get it back that way, Joel," Ruby said.

"I know. Well, I'm hungry. Let's go eat." He took a few steps.

Drake hurried to his side and took his arm. Ruby reached for her purse that hung over the chair, telling Red in her best baby voice they'd be back soon. She left a light on for him, then locked the door behind them.

It was a weeknight and yet Polly's was full of hungry eaters. A hot evening such as this, no one wanted to cook, and eating at Polly's was like eating at your mom's or a dear friend's house.

The small eatery had a few picnic tables outside under a weathered pergola with a steel roof. Inside were about twelve tables, the red vinyl seats having seen better days, now duct-taped in various places to hold the rips together.

They had to wait about fifteen minutes for one of the booths, but Drake and Ruby decided air conditioning would be better for Joel.

They studied the menus in silence. Ruby already knew what she was ordering but looked it over just the same. She closed it and set it beside her arm. She clasped her hands and smiled.

"Joel, how have you been?"

He peered at her over the menu. "Fine," he said, his gaze lowering back to the menu.

"Good," Ruby said.

"What looks appetizing, Dad?"

"I think I'll have the beer-battered cod. You don't think the little alcohol will go to my head, do you?" He flashed a grin to Drake, then folded his menu, laying it on top of Ruby's.

"Why don't you live dangerously tonight. Order a beer to go with your beer-battered fish." Drake leaned into his dad and touched his shoulder with his.

"Sounds good," Joel said.

"And for you, Ruby?" Drake held her gaze, her heart racing at full throttle.

For goodness sake's, Ruby. He just asked you what you were having for dinner, not to be your lifelong partner. She laughed. "Shrimp and grits."

"Me too!"

"I sort of figured you would."

Suddenly, a young girl came with her pad and pen. She seemed to be about twenty-one, bright-eyed, long lashes with lots of mascara, glossy, plump lips and long brown hair tied up in a red bow. She wore a white blouse, khaki shorts, and her name tag read Molly.

"What can I get you," she said, batting her lashes at Drake.

"The lady first," he said, nodding toward Ruby.

Ruby quickly turned her frown to a smile. "Shrimp and grits, and a small Stella Artois, please."

"For you sir," she said, looking at Joel.

"Beer-battered fish and chips and a small Bud, please."

She jotted down the order.

"I'll have the same as the lady. Thank you."

She reached down and grabbed the menus, hurrying away.

While they waited for their drinks, Joel told them about Mrs. Parker getting into it with one of the residents. Ruby laughed as she pictured Hazel wiggling her finger in the face of one of the residents.

"I hope they were able to mend their differences?" Ruby asked.

"Oh yeah. All is well at Shady Grove Place."

"Has the work begun on the pool yet?"

"Some guy was out measuring. I'm not really sure what's going on with that."

Drinks came out, and Joel took a long draw of his cold beer. "Cold and refreshing." He wiped the foam from his mouth.

"Glad you are enjoying it, Dad. I figure one beer can't hurt."

As they ate, they did little conversing. Everyone seemed to be enjoying the food.

Drake leaned back and patted his waist. "I'm so full. Wow was it ever good, though."

"I think we'll need a to-go box for your dad's dinner."

Drake looked over to his Dad's plate. "The portions are large here, huh Dad?"

Joel shrugged. "I should have left the fries and hush puppies alone. But they were so tasty." A low belly laugh rolled from within deep, setting Drake and Ruby to laughing too.

With Ruby on one side and Drake on the other, they escorted Joel to the car. Ruby held the Styrofoam container holding Joel's food. When they got to Shady

Grove Place, Ruby said she'd wait for them in the car. She had Drake roll down her window so she could get a whiff of the night air. She could smell the ocean even though it was a few miles away.

Drake suddenly opened the door, startling her just a little and bringing her out of her daydream.

"All settled in. He'll sleep great tonight."

"I think I'll sleep great too. Carbs." She flashed a grin.

"Yeah, good old carbs. Can't live with them, can't live without them." He started the engine.

They gingerly stepped up to the porch, trying to sneak by Red. One small bark from inside made them chuckle.

"The guard dog," Drake said.

"For real." She unlocked the door.

Red ran up to Drake and sniffed him, then waited for Ruby to pet him. Once he got what he wanted, he trotted to his bed, facing them with his front paws crossed.

"Wine?" She walked to the cupboard.

"A small glass. I'm pretty full and sort of tired. I still have a long drive back."

. . .

Uh-oh. What does that mean? She drew in her lip. *I hope he's not hinting around.* "I'm sort of tired too. Whenever I eat—"

"Carbs…" he said, finishing her sentence.

"We could always do a raincheck on wine and dessert?" She turned toward him.

"If you don't mind. That works for me. I have an early day tomorrow. The partners and I have a big case we're working on." He leaned down and patted Red on the head.

She rubbed her arms, feeling the night breeze. After a warm day, it felt refreshing, and she welcomed it. The waves were crashing onto the shore, and the whitecaps could be seen from the glow of her porch light.

"I could sleep out here and be rocked to sleep by the sounds of the ocean." His sexy smile made her shudder.

"I have slept out here before." She nodded toward the hammock. "It's so peaceful."

"I had a great time at dinner. Dad really enjoyed getting out. Thanks for thinking of him." He stepped closer.

"Oh, gosh, Drake. It was nothing. I'm happy to visit with your dad. He's a nice guy."

"So, Saturday is the big day." He rocked back on his heels.

"Yes. I'll be setting up Friday night if you want to come by and help, but that's only if you have time." She crossed her arms and hugged herself.

"I don't know. I'll see. But I'll definitely be here Saturday." He turned to take the steps down to the beach level.

"Drake," she called out.

He twisted around.

"I had a great time. I know we've both said that. It's beginning to sound like a broken record, but I just really had a great time." She hunched her shoulders and flashed a wide grin.

He traveled up the few steps and slipped his hands around her waist.

Her pounding heart along with shaky legs consumed her. She swallowed hard. Then she posed for the kiss by lifting her chin slightly, while her gaze floated down from his to his full lips. She moved in closer. Their lips touched, making the hair on the back of her neck crawl. She closed her eyes tightly, leaning into him more. His hands moved down, resting on her hips as he kissed her, a bolt of electricity shooting through her body like one of the summer lightning storms.

CHAPTER 10

She could barely concentrate. That kiss. It was something else. The chemistry they had was off the charts. Maybe it was the beer they had at dinner. Maybe it was the romantic feel of the ocean air on the porch. She shook her head as she went over the kiss step by step and everything that led up to it.

She got out her sewing machine to stitch up the last six bandannas. She turned on some music, poured herself a glass of iced tea and continued to work on the bandannas. She'd saved some of the cutest fabric designs for last. She giggled when she imagined some little dog wearing the bright green one that said, "sock thief," or the Halloween-themed one with pumpkins, scary black cats and haunted houses, or the Christmas one with Santa Claus, or in honor of St. Patrick's Day, one with four-leaf clovers on them. It took her no time to get them ready to add to the already finished ones.

Unexpectedly, her phone chimed. It was Mrs. Parker.

"Hey, Mrs. Parker."

"Listen. They just took Joel Carrolton out of here in an ambulance. I thought you should know."

"Oh no! Does Drake know?"

"I just called him, but it went into voice mail."

"Okay. Let me think. I don't know where he lives. I just have his phone number too. I'll go to the hospital. I don't want Joel alone. You keep trying to reach Drake."

She grabbed her purse and ran out of the house, leaving on the lights and music and her iced tea sitting. She dialed his number while she frantically drove to the hospital. Each time it went into voicemail. "Gaw!" she yelled, driving faster.

She entered the emergency side of the hospital, out of breath. "I'm here because you brought my friend in. Joel Carrolton."

The nurse looked at her computer screen.

"Please, I'm a friend of his. We can't get ahold of his son."

"He's in an examination room being checked out now."

"What can you tell me. Why was he brought here? I need something to tell Drake. His son, Drake," Ruby said, holding on to the reception desk.

"He complained of his chest hurting and shortness of breath."

Ruby leaned her head back and looked up. She lowered her gaze to the nurse working the desk. "Okay. Thank you. I'll just be sitting over here." She reared up from the desk and motioned toward the row of chairs near the window.

As she waited for word about Joel, she kept trying Drake's number. Finally, after four attempts he answered. "I'm on the way. I just got Mrs. Parker's message. Is he… is he alive?"

"Yes. I haven't heard anything about his condition. Please hurry. Be safe, though, Drake. I want you in one piece."

After about twenty minutes, a doctor came out. He smiled as he moved closer to her. "I understand you're Joel's friend?" He sat beside her.

His soft, leveled voice and the look in his eye gave her concern. Was he about to give her bad news?

Ruby swallowed silently. Trying to steady her voice to match his, she replied, "Yes. My name is Ruby Bennett. I've known Joel for a few years. His son Drake is on the way."

"He's resting comfortably. We are going to take him up to x-ray for some tests. He may have some blockage. When do you think his son will arrive?"

"He's coming from Orlando."

The doctor nodded, then peered at his watch. "Okay, so he's a distance away." He stood, towering over her.

Ruby looked him squarely in the eyes. "I'm sure he'll tell you to do what is necessary to help him, but I can't authorize anything."

"That's all well and good, but Joel has a DNR in his medical records. So, although he is willing to receive care, he doesn't want any advanced cardiac life support or those kinds of resuscitations."

Ruby folded her arms and lowered her eyes.

The doctor reached out and comforted her by resting his hand on her arm. "We'll take a look and see what's going on. Hopefully, we have some time to figure things out. When his son comes in, please have him check in with the nurse."

Ruby sat holding her face in her hands. She leaned back and brushed her hands through her hair. How could this happen? Everything was going so well. She tried to look at the television, but all she saw was blobs of flesh and lips moving. She tried to look at a magazine but instead flipped pages. When Drake rushed in, she'd never been so happy to see anyone in her life. She jumped up and flung her body into his arms.

"Where is he?" He held her back, a look of sheer worry on his face.

"They took him up for some tests. The doctor said for you to check in with the nurse."

Ruby watched as he hurried over to the desk. She couldn't make out everything he said, but she heard the words, my dad and Drake. She hugged her arms as she paced the waiting room. Finally, Drake joined her.

"Are you okay?" He put his arm around her and held her tight.

"No. I don't know how I'm feeling. I just don't understand."

"Dad's not a young man, Ruby. He's seventy-five years old."

"That's not old." She pushed her lips out in a pout, then reached up and wiped the tears away that slid down her face.

"No, but he doesn't get much exercise, and the fish and chips probably weren't the best thing for him to eat. But I hate always telling him what he can and can't eat."

"I know," she said, followed by a sigh.

"Mr. Carrolton."

Drake turned around.

The doctor that spoke with Ruby walked over and extended his hand.

"I spoke with your dad's friend earlier." He tipped his head toward Ruby. "The tests reveal your dad has quite a bit of blockage in a couple of his arteries. What we would like to do is insert a stent. Are you familiar with this procedure?"

"I've heard of it before," Drake said.

"It's quite a normal procedure actually. What we'll do is insert a stent into the clogged artery with a balloon catheter. The catheter is inflated, and the stent expands and locks in place."

"How long will he be in the hospital, and do you feel he can handle this type of procedure all right?"

"Well, as I told Ms. Bennett, your dad has a DNR on file. If something were to happen while we were putting in the stent, we'd have to obey his wishes. I can tell you only about one percent ever become life-threatening. I feel your dad is in good shape, and we'll do everything in our power to make it a success. He should be able to go home in twenty-four hours or so."

Drake shot Ruby a look. Ruby returned his surprised look with a friendly smile.

"I'll come back out and update you with details and his progress soon. You might want to go to the second floor to the cardio unit and wait there."

The doctor walked away, leaving Drake and Ruby alone with their deepest thoughts and fears.

Ruby reached out to touch Drake. He pulled away, crossing his arms. What was that about, she wondered? Time. He needed that and space.

"Listen, now that you're here I should be going. You don't need me." She took a few steps toward the glass door.

He didn't respond.

"Call me if you need anything," she said, closer to leaving the waiting room than she really wanted, if she were to be completely honest. "I'll say a prayer for Joel." She put her hand on the bar to open the door.

"Ruby," he said, barely above a whisper. If she hadn't been stretching her ear for any sounds, she might not have heard it. She whirled around.

"Yes, Drake?"

"Please don't go."

She let go of the silver bar, releasing it. She made a few steps toward him, stopping just short of him. "Are you sure?"

He walked up to her and slipped his hands around her waist, leaning in toward her ear. "I've never been more sure about anything in my life."

She rested her chin on his broad shoulder, her gaze skimming around as she processed these words. Were they talking about the same thing? "I'll stay," she said, reaching up and gently stroking his back.

CHAPTER 11

*D*rake and Ruby rode the elevator to the second floor in silence. She didn't dare ask him how he was feeling. But what do you say in times like this? Thankfully she didn't have to wait in the emergency waiting room any longer, but the cardio unit waiting room felt even more dire if that were possible. People huddled in corners whispering and crying brought back all kinds of memories of when her parents were killed.

Drake had been gone for almost an hour. She hated not knowing what was going on. Her stomach pitched and rolled, and her mouth was dry from the three cups of coffee she'd consumed, she needed water. Soon she'd need a bathroom. Thank goodness for a good bladder.

Quickly, the door to the other rooms opened and out came Drake.

Her gaze darted around his face as she tried to read him.

He drew in a big breath and let it out loudly. "Dad's in recovery. Everything went well. He's already coming out of the anesthesia and asking to go home." He pulled her in and whirled her around, lifting her feet off the ground.

"That's great news, Drake. I'm so happy for you and for him. When can I see him?"

"Doc said give them a little more time. They'll come out to get us."

Get us. She liked the way that sounded. The way it rolled off his tongue so naturally. Us. Was there really an us?

A nurse came out and called them to the door.

Drake took Ruby's hand and led the way.

"Now, he's still a bit groggy. Saying some things like he wants to go swimming and have a beer, but for the most part, I think Joel Carrolton is here." The nurse laughed as she led the way to his room.

She let Drake enter the room first. She clasped her hands and walked to the end of his bed. His face, pale as ever, and the dreaded beeping machines nearby reminded her what she didn't like about hospitals.

"Dad. It's me and Ruby. We're here." He touched his dad's forearm with caution.

Joel mumbled, then licked his mouth. "Thirsty," he said.

The nurse had already instructed Drake to only give Joel ice chips.

Ruby watched as Drake carefully placed the cup to his father's mouth. "Sorry, Dad, all you can have is ice chips."

His eyes flew open, startling Ruby. She gasped, then a nervous giggle escaped her mouth. "Hey, Joel. It's Ruby. I'm here too."

He tried to lift his hand to wave.

"Listen, Dad, you probably need some rest. The doctor says just an overnight stay is all you need. I'll be back tomorrow to get you."

"Okay," he said.

Ruby ducked out of the room to give Drake and his dad a few private moments. She rested her back up against the wall and watched the lively unit with nurses and doctors coming and going. She admired what they did, but she couldn't wait to get out into the fresh air. Even if it was ninety degrees and eighty percent humidity.

The door flew open, and Drake came out. She looked for signs. Signs of anything. Were those tears? She held her breath as he approached.

"He'll be okay. He's in great hands. I'm out here watching this crew. They're so professional and right on it. I know he's in the best of care." She looped her arm with his.

He nodded. "How about we go get something to eat?"

"As long as it isn't hospital food, I'm game." She pulled him close, hugging his arm. She wasn't prepared for what came next.

He leaned over and kissed her.

HE WALKED her to her car, releasing her hand as she dug for her key fob.

"Follow me. I know this little place we can grab a sandwich and a cold drink." She clicked the button to unlock her doors.

His mind was all over the place as he followed her to the restaurant. With his dad living in Shady Grove, maybe living in Orlando wasn't working. Joel needed him more as he was getting older, and now with this health thing. Besides, Ruby was too far away from him too. He wanted to see her more often. Then he thought about her warm lips. He wondered how many men had the pleasure of kissing her? If they had, wouldn't they still be with her? She drew him right in and made him never want to leave. Made him shudder, and for a man, that was a big deal, right? Her trim and petite body, the way she laughed, and the way she held his gaze. It was enough to cause him to drop to his knees.

They pulled into the parking lot, and he took a second to gather his thoughts. *Do I dare tell her she makes me crazy, that lately all I can think about is her? That it takes everything in me to not pull her in and kiss her nonstop? No, I can't tell her that, can I?*

"Have you been here before?"

"No, I haven't." He took her hand in his and squeezed it.

"Good. A new place for us."

Us. Us. Us.

They ordered a plate of nachos and two frosty mugs of beer. They agreed they deserved it after what Joel had been through.

"Poor Joel," she said, sipping her frothy mug.

"Dad's tough as nails. He's gonna bounce right back. You wait and see." He dragged a corn chip stacked high with shredded chicken, sour cream, and guacamole out of the pile and stuffed it into his mouth.

"While I was waiting for you, Mrs. Parker called. She wanted an update to give to the residents."

"Good," he said, nodding.

"She also told me they've started on the resurfacing of the pool. And get this," she said smiling car to ear, "someone has donated one of those chairs that people with disabilities can use at the pool. They're harnessed in and lowered into the pool. That way they can get some benefit of the water."

"Wow. That's fabulous. Those aren't cheap."

"And the news keeps getting better. The city is coming out and free of charge going to trim those huge palm trees that line the sidewalk out in front, and they are going to fix the cracked sidewalk."

"You're right. The news just keeps getting better." He drew the mug to his lips.

"I've got one more bit of news." She wiggled her brows up and down then giggled.

"Hit me," he said, chuckling back.

"Home Depot has donated a new automatic front door."

"Man, that's great, Ruby. You know you deserve so much praise for this. You're the one that got the ball rolling with the renovations and improvements." He reached his hand out across the table.

She lowered her eyes to his hand, sliding hers forward. He laced his fingers with hers. "Ruby, there's something I want to tell you."

His stomach clenched tightly, wondering if this was the right time. His heart kicked up a few beats, and he could feel the pulse in his neck throb.

"You're scaring me. What is it?"

"Oh, I didn't mean to scare you. I just wanted to tell you how much you mean to me." He picked up her hand, rubbing imaginary circles on her palm.

She closed her eyes. He watched her for any signs of rebuttal. This was crazy stuff right here, telling a girl you've only met how much you care for her. "Too soon?"

The corners of her mouth drew up, setting his mind a little more at ease that maybe, just maybe, she felt the same way.

"When you said us, it sent me into a tailspin. I wasn't sure if you meant us as in couple or just us as you and me hanging out…"

He drew her hands to his mouth and kissed it. "Shh."

She blinked a few times.

"I meant us as in you and me, a couple, together, in it for the long haul and anything else you might want to label it."

"I'm so happy you clarified that," she snickered.

"You had me at the kiss, Ruby Bennett."

"You had me before that," she said, her eyes never wavering from his.

CHAPTER 12

To say that was the turning point in their relationship would be an understatement. Of course, it was! Ruby kept busy with the final preparations for the sale. She'd set up all the tables and decorated them with bright vinyl tablecloths she'd picked up at the dollar store nearby, setting the books out for display. She categorized all the romance together, cozy mysteries in another section, and the few miscellaneous genres in another.

The bake sale table had cupcakes, cookies, and brownies all wrapped in colorful cellophane with small index cards showing the item and price. Mrs. Parker offered to man that table since Joel couldn't, or shouldn't.

"Joel, you must not overdo it. The doctor said no exertion." Mrs. Parker could be heard from afar barking out orders to Joel.

After Ruby listened to it for a bit, she intervened.

"Mrs. Parker, why don't you go check on the lemonade." She coaxed her to move along toward the kitchen.

"Thank you," Joel said, clearly exhausted by Mrs. Parker's well-intentioned concern.

"No problem. Have you heard from Drake today?" Ruby tried to make her questioning seem out of curiosity and nothing else. No need to get Joel all worked up about anything.

"Yes, he said he's running late. Apparently, he got a visit from some old girlfriend." Joel chuckled.

Ruby tilted her head and widened her eyes, not sure how to respond.

"He's coming though. He told me to let you know." Joel held on to his walker and moved slowly away from Ruby.

"Joel."

He stopped but didn't turn around.

Ruby rushed alongside him, finally coming around the front of his walker.

"How'd he sound? I mean was he upset by her dropping by?" The heck with curiosity. She wanted to know details.

"I couldn't detect anything. Seemed normal to me." He shuffled a few steps, almost running her over. She jumped out of his way and watched him go.

"Remember what the doctor said. No exertion."

He lifted his hand and gave her a backhanded wave. "Not you too," he grumbled.

THE TOWNSPEOPLE CAME out in droves, showing their support of Ruby and Shady Grove Place. The baked goods went fast, and until she marked the books down, they were a bit slower to move. But once she reduced the price, they started selling too.

One of the resident's granddaughters manned the lemonade stand, and another's helped give tours of the facility. Ruby looked at her phone. No missed calls. The phone said it was three o'clock. The bake sale was almost over and still no Drake. She pushed back into her chair and crossed her arms. She chewed on the corner of her mouth as she pondered what her next move was. Surely he had a good explanation as to why he missed the event.

She saw his car pull around back of Shady Grove Place. She could feel her temper rising and the blood rushing to her cheeks. She tried to steady her anger and let him explain. She owed him that much.

"Sorry I'm late, Ruby." He leaned over and dropped a kiss on her forehead.

Her jaw tightened.

He looked over to the bake sale table, and all that was left were crumbs. Then his gaze traveled to the books. A few remained. "Looks like you did pretty well today." He pulled up a chair and sat next to her.

"Yeah, not too bad," she said through clenched teeth.

He rested his hand on her knee. "I better go say hi to Dad." He dropped another kiss, this time on the top of her head.

Okay, that's strange. No mention of why he was late. She stood and began to stack the few books left and rearrange a few others.

She heard him laugh, and in the pit of her stomach, she ached. He came up behind her and slid his arms around her. "You look beautiful today," he whispered in her ear.

She tensed up and swallowed. "Thanks."

"What's wrong?" He turned her around to face him.

She refused to look him in the eye. She didn't want to give anything away.

"Ruby?" He lifted her chin with his finger.

"Nothing." She dropped her gaze, forcing his hand away.

"I know better than that. Something is wrong. Are you going to tell me or make me guess?"

She moved away from him. The close proximity to him drove her crazy. She wanted him, but she was mad at him right now. She picked up her phone and studied it. "I'm going to start cleaning up. The sale is officially over." She dropped down, lifted the tablecloth, brought out some boxes from under the table and began to put the books in them.

"Let me help," he said, coming over to her.

"No, I got it. Why don't you go visit with your dad? He's really doing well." She still refused to make eye contact with him.

He slammed a book on the table, making her jump. "Okay, enough of the games. I told you I was sorry for being late. Are you going to punish me forever?" He ran his hand through his hair and stared off into space.

With her eyes wide as saucers, she observed him as he looked off into the distance. *Playing games?*

"When you're ready to talk, you know where I am." He walked away, going back inside to look for his dad.

A few tears trickled down her face. She quickly wiped them away as she filled the box. She lugged it to her car and put them inside. She began to tear down the tables when he came back out.

"How much money did you make today?" His voice was light and airy as if they'd not had a fight. It made it worse.

"Money? How much money? Is that all you care about?"

Now a flood of tears fell down her face, and soon she was blubbering.

He wrapped his strong arms around her and held her tight. "What's wrong?"

"Your dad said a girl dropped by your place. That's why you were late." She sobbed into his chest.

He pushed her back and studied her. She was sure her face was blotchy and red and her eyes swollen from ugly crying. "Yes, Chrissy came by to get something she'd left behind. She tried to get things going again with me, but I told her no. She was relentless at first, but when I just flat out told her she couldn't even come close to you, she left crying and that's that. Then as I was coming here, I got a flat tire. That's why I'm really late."

She brushed the tears away and stiffened her back. "A flat tire?"

He nodded.

"Why didn't you call me? Or your dad?"

"I did. I called Dad and told him to let you know I would be late."

A pinched expression came over her as she recalled the conversation with Joel.

"He did tell you, didn't he?" Now Drake had a puzzled look.

"He did," she said slowly, "but he neglected to tell me about the flat tire. Just said the girl came over."

"That's odd. Dad never gets the story wrong. Wonder if something is going on with him?"

"Medication," they both said at the same time.

They rushed inside to find Joel in his apartment passed out. Ruby immediately called 9-1-1 while Drake held a cold compress to his forehead. He came around before the ambulance showed up. They checked his vital signs and said everything was good. They determined it was his medication and after a call into the doctor, a new prescription was ordered.

"Dad, you gave us another scare." Drake slung his arm around his dad's shoulder.

Us. Us. Us.

"Yes, you did," Ruby said, sitting on the other side.

"What gave it away?" Joel asked.

"Well, you forgot to mention to Ruby about my flat tire."

"I did?"

Ruby nodded. "But that's all right. Now we know you needed a medication tweak. It's all good."

"How'd the sale go?" Joel asked.

"It went well. I haven't had a chance to count the money yet. With all the excitement and all," Ruby said.

"I promise you both, I'm not doing this for attention."

Drake leaned back and looked behind his dad's head. He got Ruby's attention by tipping his chin at her. They locked eyes. *I'm sorry*, he mouthed.

She batted her lashes a couple of times. *I'm sorry too*, she mouthed back.

"What's all that whispering going on behind my back?" Joel asked.

"Nothing, Dad," Drake said, winking at Ruby.

CHAPTER 13

"You know what the best part of an argument is?" Drake held her hand as they walked along the beach, Red running ahead trying to work out his pent-up energy.

"No, what?" They swung hands as they walked.

"This." He stopped and swooped her up into his arms, lifting her feet off the sandy beach and planting a big kiss squarely on her mouth. He sat her back down, feet firmly on the ground, his eyes twinkling at her.

"Well, in that case, we should argue more often." She slid her arm around him and snuggled into his solid frame, loving the secure feeling she got from being so close to him.

Swiftly, Red ran up. He had something in his mouth.

"Leave it," Ruby commanded.

He dropped it at her feet.

She bent over at the waist, looking at the dark brown thing with seaweed draped over it. She then kicked it. "What is that?" She glanced up at Drake with a puzzled look.

"Looks like the sole from a shoe," Drake said upon further investigation.

Red went to retrieve it once more.

"No, leave it," she said, shooing him away.

They walked a little more.

"I counted the money from the book and bake sale."

"And?" He dropped his gaze to her.

"It wasn't what I wanted, but I had to keep discounting books. I realized that old people really are cheap." She laughed.

"What was the end result?" he asked.

"Four hundred dollars even."

He rocked his head side to side as he thought this over. "Well, that's better than zero."

"True. I just have one more ace up my sleeve. The dog walk on the beach."

"How many bandannas did you make?"

"I made fifty. I'm going to sell them for three dollars each. So that's one hundred fifty dollars. Each entry fee is a minimum of ten dollars. I'm hoping many give more, but seems we have a lot of cheapskates here."

He lifted an interested brow. "So, you said. How many people signed up?"

"I have eighty registered, but I said on the flyer that people were welcome to come out and support the event at any time."

"Looks like you could bring in a thousand bucks." He pursed his lips and nodded.

"A thousand for the dog walk, four hundred for the book and bake sale for a total of fourteen hundred dollars. Added to your ten thousand dollars we're six hundred dollars short."

"Don't throw in the towel just yet. You never know what someone might donate for the dog walk. But just in case we are short, what other event can you come up with at this late date?"

She managed a wry smile. "Yeah, right."

His hazel eyes danced with amusement, making her heart skip a beat.

"No, seriously. Don't you have one other thing you can pull out of your hat and send us straight to the finish line? Like six hundred dollars' worth?"

They walked along in silence, enjoying the sunset. The glowing sun dipped down as if it were riding on top of the ocean. The light cast from it beamed across the water as it pirouetted along a path to shore. The vivid colors of red, orange, and blue lit up the vast darkness above, creating a watercolor picture that took their breath away.

The sounds of the waves rolling in and out gave them a feeling of stillness, and when Drake stopped and stared deep into her eyes, she drifted back into his hold and closed her eyes, dropping her hands to her side. The warmth of his mouth on hers made her stomach clench with anticipation, and just below her stomach, another sort of sensation occurred. This was serious stuff right here. These feelings could not be dismissed. He gently eased her mouth open as he gingerly teased her with his tongue. She moaned softly. Unexpectedly, she felt a wet tongue on her dangling hand.

"Red," she yelled.

Drake fell out laughing so hard over Red's interruption. "More of this later," he said in a low, sexy tone that tugged at her heartstrings and elsewhere.

"A dance on the beach," she said flatly.

His reflective gaze searched her face. "A dance on the beach?"

"You know. An old-fashioned dance, bonfire, music, food and drinks?"

"You mean like shag dancing?" He cocked his head.

"Well, that's what they do in South Carolina, but here in Florida, we have the Latina flair. We can have a temporary wooden dance floor put down here at the beach, we can light up the area with tiki torches. It will be a blast!" The enthusiasm in her voice rose with each idea.

"Good thing Mr. Jensen got an extension," Drake said. "How can I help?"

THE WHEELS WERE SET into motion that night on the beach. Not just for the last attempt in raising money for Shady Grove Place, but for Ruby and Drake.

A few phone calls later and Ruby had a temporary dance floor reserved, a local band lined up, a food truck ready to deliver delicious food, and someone to man the keg of beer and wine table—both of which were provided by a local restaurant with the promise of paying for them afterward. Ruby calculated how much each plastic cup of beer or wine would cost in order to recoup the price of the alcohol. The band graciously donated their time with the understanding they could sell their current CD. The food truck would keep their profits. Ruby had to sell the idea by selling tickets to the event, around six hundred dollars' worth.

Drake and Ruby came up with the dollar amount for the dance. A minimum donation of twenty-five dollars per couple or ten dollars for a single. It was a gamble, but one they both knew they had to take.

They only had a few days to put it on, and it would come on the heels of the dog event. Nothing said Save Shady Grove Place like a succession of charity events to keep the enthusiasm going, and it just might work!

"OKAY, SO THIS IS THE PLAN." Ruby rubbed her forehead, a sigh escaping her lips.

"You're going to need a vacation after all of this," Drake said, his eyes crinkling in the corners.

"Let's stay focused. I have everything set up for the dance tonight after the dog walk. My hope is that everyone will stick around for the dance, or at the least, come back. I've exhausted all of my favors I'm afraid. Everyone has been so nice about donating their time and things to get this going."

"I always say go big or go home." Drake's warm fingers brushed against her hand.

Goose bumps ran rampant with his touch. "Thank you for helping me. I couldn't have done it without you."

"We haven't succeeded yet. Save your thank-yous until later."

EVERYONE HAD an absolute blast at the dog event. There were big dogs, small dogs, dogs with bows in their fur, old dogs, puppies, and the owners were just as colorful. Some owners took the event a notch further by color coordinating with their pets. T-shirts and bows, collars and leashes. So when the bandannas sold out quickly, it was no surprise. These owners loved their pets. An array of pets running down the sandy beaches, catching Frisbees tossed into the air, running the obstacle course they set up, and running to the finish line. Groups of spectators watched as the dogs entertained beachgoers of every age. It put a smile on Ruby's face, that's for certain.

Ruby worked the ticket table like it was life or death. She sold tickets to the dance to every person who came to the dog event. Every single one. And the few who said they couldn't come back tossed in money anyway. But the big surprise came when she counted the money later that afternoon in between the two events. Unbeknownst to her, someone tossed in a hundred-dollar bill. She scrunched the bill between her fingers, feeling the paper. Then she tossed it into the large coffee can with the rest.

She picked up her phone and held it. She had exactly three hours before the event. She rested her head back and closed her eyes. Just for a moment.

Her eyes flew open from the pounding at the front door. "Ruby. Ruby."

She jogged to the door and pulled it open. Drake stood on the porch. "What time is it?" She ran her hand through her hair.

"You have exactly twenty minutes to get ready. I wondered why you weren't out here yet. People are gathering, the band is setting up, and Chimmey is cooking up shrimp, chicken strips, and all the rest."

"Chimmey? Oh, the owner of the Shrimp Mobile. Gotcha. Okay, I'll take the fastest shower known to man. Meet you outside in a few. Take Red with you. I'll be out soon."

She jumped in for a fast rinse off, deciding there was no time for a shampoo, and threw on her clothes. Thankfully, she'd laid out the summer dress she was to wear. Pulling her hair up into a twist, she secured it with bobby pins and stuck the artificial flower barrette in place, hoping it would be enough to disguise her unwashed hair. She gave herself a quick look over before dashing outside.

She gazed high and low into the sea of people. She located Drake, making a beeline toward him. Her feet suddenly dug into the sand, and she almost toppled over when someone grabbed her elbow, stopping her. She whirled around and made eye contact with a tall man wearing a Hawaiian print shirt, stubble on his chin, and bloodshot eyes. Someone had been hitting the keg already.

"Hey pretty lady, wanna dance?" He twirled her around and around, then slipped his hands around her waist, tugging her forward.

She put up her hand and held him at bay. With only a few inches separating them, she could smell the heavy beer breath. "Listen, I'm looking for someone." She tried to wiggle out of his clutches.

"And you found him, pretty lady." He reeled her back in.

"No, you don't understand," she said, craning her neck to see if anyone could save her.

"Aw, come on. Dance with me." He reached for her hand and spun her around.

She got a glimpse of Drake and Red. They were walking toward her but oblivious to what was taking place. She kept her eyes focused on them, hoping he'd look her way. Hastily, her new friend swung her around, dipping her in another surprise move. With her head level to the sand, all she could see was feet and legs. As he pulled her up, she locked eyes with Drake.

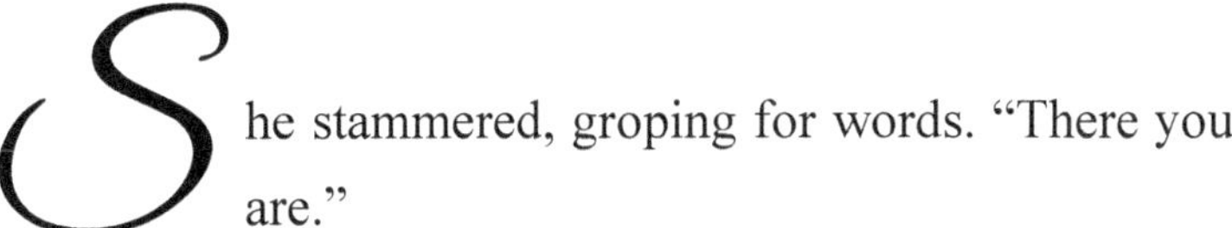

CHAPTER 14

She stammered, groping for words. "There you are."

Drake bounced his gaze from her to the drunk guy, finally resting back on her. "Am I interrupting something?"

"No, not at all." She pulled herself out of the man's clutches, looping her arm in Drake's. "This guy," she said, giving Drake the *save me* look, "was just showing me a couple of dance moves."

Drake bobbled his head around her and looked the guy up and down. Then turning back to her he said, "Is he bothering you?"

She shrugged and winced. "But it's no problem. He's had a little bit too much to drink," she whispered.

"Hey, you didn't finish the dance with me," the drunk guy said, wobbling toward her.

Drake put out his arm and caught the guy just below the throat. "She doesn't want to dance with you. Get lost." He shoved the guy backward.

The guy lost his balance and fell into the sand. Red barked, and soon a crowd of people gathered around them.

"It's okay, folks. Nothing to see here," she said, trying to push them back to minding their own business.

The guy slowly stood, brushing the sand off his legs. "That wasn't cool," he sputtered, then wiped his mouth.

"What you're doing isn't cool either. Go get some coffee." Drake turned and put his arm around Ruby and began to walk away.

"Hey," a voice said.

She felt a jerk, and soon after she and Drake both were jolted backward, sending her to the ground and Drake off-balance.

Then the drunk guy sucker-punched Drake.

Screams and yells came from the crowd along with several barking dogs. Red got in on the action by growling at the drunk.

Rubbing his sore jaw, Drake reached for Ruby's hand and helped her up off the ground while keeping eyes on the guy.

"Let's just go," Ruby pleaded.

"Either I finish this, or the police do. Which do you want?" A sharp look under his brows sent a wave of concern through her.

She stepped back.

Drake took two steps toward the guy, with balled-up fists. Suddenly, two other guys came out of the crowd. Friends of the drunk guy.

"So now it's going to be three against one? Where's the fairness in that?" Drake relaxed his hands.

"He's drunk. He doesn't know what he's doing. We'll take him home."

"Good. Because I was about to clean his clock." Drake rubbed his hand along his jaw.

"No worries, dude. We got it." The guys pulled the obnoxious guy away from the scene.

Ruby ran up to Drake and cuddled him. "Oh, Drake. I'm so sorry that happened. Let's get some ice on that." She led him over to the beverage table. She held ice chips to his jaw while water dripped down her hand and wrist.

"I'm fine," he said, moving away from her doctoring.

"Are you sure? You're probably going to have a big bruise."

"Better than a broken jaw. That guy, even in his drunkenness, could throw a decent punch." He chuckled, then touched his jaw again.

"Thanks for coming to my aid. I probably could have handled it differently."

Drake dropped his hands to his side. "Let me get this straight. You don't approve of the way I handled the situation?" He narrowed his eyes.

"No, it's not that. We women would—"

"Oh, I get it. Don't like violence? Well, if you wanted him to parade you around like some doll, then have at it." He stormed off.

Red had no clue they were arguing. He started running to catch up with Drake.

Ruby's eyes welled up, and soon the big crowds were nothing but a big blur. She headed back over to the beverage table and asked for a glass of wine. And instead of moving back into the crowd, she finished it right there. After she guzzled it down, she held out her plastic tumbler. "And another, please."

Now she'd had two glasses of wine. Anyone who knew Ruby Bennett knew she was a two-glass girl. In other words, a lightweight. Top it with her anger over the situation, and she was more than just a bit tipsy. The more she thought about Drake storming off, the more it made her blood boil.

"Excuse me," she said, making her way through the heavy crowd of partiers.

"Hey, Ruby. Great party," someone called out.

She gave them a wave and kept merging through.

"Want to dance?" some guy yelled at her, followed by laughing.

She flew the bird at him.

Finally, her gaze settled on Drake leaning against the food truck sipping on a beer.

She gulped, then proceeded.

"What are you doing here? Don't you have a dance partner waiting for you somewhere?" His snide remark cut her to the core.

"Don't be childish, Drake Carrolton." She turned and leaned up against the truck beside him.

"Me, childish? I think you've got that backwards."

"I don't like violence," she said, her words coming out high-pitched a result of the wine.

"I only resort to it if someone I deeply care about is being wronged." He drew in another taste of his beer, his eyes focused straight ahead.

"Can we start over?" She cuddled up next to him, brushing his arm with hers.

He pursed his lips tightly then moaned.

"What?"

"Nothing. My jaw is just a bit sore."

She raised up on her tippy toes and kissed his jaw. She stayed raised while kissing his mouth. "I'm sorry, Drake."

He dropped his gaze, not saying a word but staring at her coldly.

"Please say something." She lowered herself and rested back against the truck. "I need another glass of wine." She tapped her head against the metal truck.

He walked away from her, leaving her standing there. She watched with careful eyes, her anger building back up. She crossed her arms and huffed. She watched him toss his empty beer cup into the trash can. Turning slightly away, he rolled his finger toward her to follow him. She pushed off from the truck and hurried to him.

The band began again after a fifteen-minute break, and the people were cheering, laughing, and dancing. Drake led her around the back of the stage, trying to escape the loud music so they could talk.

"I guess I did go kind of caveman on him," Drake yelled over the music.

"Well, he wasn't acting exactly gentleman-like."

"This is a good turnout," he said, nodding toward the noise.

Ruby looked around him and saw in the distance a tall sand dune. "Come on." She tugged at his hand, then clasped his fingers with hers.

They laughed as they kicked up sand, seeking shelter. The sand acted as a great sound barrier. "Thanks for coming to my rescue." She puckered her lips for a kiss.

He tapped a quick kiss to her lips. "No worries."

She dropped to her bottom at the base of the dune, sending him spiraling down with her. A small wine-induced giggle escaped her lips. She leaned against the mound, listening to the music shoot over them and the cheerful banter of the people. "Such a beautiful night." She pulled her gaze up to the sky, marveling at the stars.

He rested a hand on her leg. "You look pretty in that sundress. And by the way, how many glasses of wine have you had?"

His voice had a warm touch, giving off a sudden sensation of startling sweetness. "Thank you. I guess not as much as the drunk guy had, but then, I'm a lightweight. Just ask anyone." She tossed her head back and laughed.

Drake shook his head in a slow, dramatic shake. "I should probably get you home."

The band played a slow song with words that described just how she'd been feeling. It stirred up emotions deep inside. She drew circles on Drake's palm while resting one hand on his knee.

"Is this the kind of thing you write about in your books?" He lowered his alluring eyes to her, obviously forgetting that some of this might be due to her giddy feeling.

"Yeah. Everyone loves to read about romance."

He dropped a kiss on her forehead.

"Drake?"

"Yep."

"After we get Shady Grove Place up and running again, do you think we'll still be together?"

"Sure, why not?"

She let out a slow exhale. "I just wondered."

He lifted her chin with his finger while gazing deeply into her eyes. She noticed the yellow flecks in his eyes as the nearby tiki torch flickered. "I've been thinking about maybe moving closer to the beach."

She sucked in a soft, shocked breath. "Seriously?"

He leaned in, finding her mouth quickly without any resistance. She groaned softly, letting him know he was pleasing her. Trailing kisses along her neck, he soon reached her earlobes, melting her into a shivering bundle of human flesh. She pulled back slightly, catching her breath and cupping his face to stop the torture. A coy grin emerged on his face, and in one fell swoop, he slipped his fingers through her hair, holding her steady as he moved in for more.

THEY HELD each other tight as they both waved good-bye to Chimmey. His truck rattled and rocked as it drove off the compressed sand and made its way to the street. Then they walked over to the band who were finishing up, putting their instruments and equipment away.

"Thanks again for playing, guys." Ruby settled into Drake's shoulder, now feeling the crash of coming down from her little buzz from the wine.

"Anytime," the leader said.

Once the band and food truck were gone, all that was left was the wooden dance floor, the tiki torches, and a few folding tables.

Ruby watched as Drake headed for the dance floor. He opened his arms wide.

She giggled as she walked toward him.

"Would you have this dance with me?" The corners of his mouth drew up in a sexy smile.

She moved into his hold, and they started swaying to the sounds of the ocean waves as they rolled in and rolled out, with the flames of the torches flickering in the breeze. Ruby laid her head on his chest and prayed this night would never end.

CHAPTER 15

"I'll come back in the morning and help clean up the beach. I think you should go to bed. It's been a long day." He wrapped his arm around her shoulder as they walked toward the little cottage with white lights lining the porch.

"You'll drive all the way home and come back?"

"No, I'm going to crash over at Dad's place. I'll take him out for breakfast, then head over. Unless you'd like to join us for breakfast too?"

"Food doesn't sound good right now." She held her hand to her stomach.

"Too much wine?"

"And nothing to eat."

"Well, I'll call you in the morning. You can tell me then." He stopped at her door.

"Do you want to come in?" Her words were inviting, but the tone said otherwise.

"No," he said, chuckling. "You and Red call it a night." He dropped a kiss on her forehead, but when he pulled back, she held him by wrapping her arms around his neck.

"Drake?"

He gave her a concerned look. "Yes?"

"I'm sorry I got angry with you. I should have let you punch that guy."

"No, I'm glad you diffused the situation. Nothing good would have come from it."

"I'm glad his friends showed up when they did," she said.

"Yeah, I wasn't sure how that was going to go down. But I had my cell phone ready to call the police."

Red pawed at the door.

"Well, guess someone else is tired. Good night." She opened the door.

"I'll call you in the morning." He waved, stepping backward off into the sand.

He sat in his car for a moment, running his hand through his hair. It would be so easy to take advantage of her. But that wasn't his way of doing things. If they were to be together that way, he wanted her fully aware of everything that was taking place. Afterward, they'd celebrate with wine. He tipped his head, then leaning forward, cranked the engine and turned the tunes up. "I sure hope Dad is still awake."

"Thanks for letting me crash here tonight." Drake rolled a sheet out onto the small sofa and fluffed a pillow.

"No problem, Son. Is everything okay?"

"Yes, the event went well. I think we raised enough money to help Mr. Jensen pay his back taxes and maybe with some left over."

"But who punched you and why?" He tipped his chin toward Drake's face.

Drake ran his hand across his jaw. "Oh that. Well how about I tell you over breakfast. When I'm thinking clearly."

"Okay, Son. Good night." He shuffled toward his bedroom.

"Dad?" Drake called out.

Joel stopped and turned.

"Do you mind if we pick up Ruby tomorrow morning for breakfast?"

"If you'd said anything else, I'd have called you a dumbass. See you in the morning."

Drake kicked off his shoes, dropped his shorts and laid them across the arm of the couch. Pulling off his shirt, he settled under the blanket. A soft glow from the night-lights in the bathroom and kitchen provided just enough light to keep his thoughts moving through his mind. Finally, he closed his eyes and drifted off to sleep.

EVEN THOUGH HE carefully folded his clothes before going to sleep, there was no denying these were the same articles of clothing he'd worn the night before. Drake watched his dad in the compact kitchen, making his coffee. He studied him carefully, then widening his eyes he yelled out, "Dad, do you have a shirt I can borrow?"

"Sure. Go check out my closet. I think I have something you can wear."

Drake searched the closet for something that didn't say old man on it. But his dad wasn't really old. His body may have shown signs of wearing down, but his spirit surely had not. He yanked a gray rayon shirt with tropical flowers off the hanger. He eyed it up and down. Tropical. Summer. "We're at the beach." He matched it with his khaki shorts. "Perfect."

Good thing his dad hoarded stuff. He found a brand-new razor and toothbrush under the bathroom sink. With a towel wrapped around him, he eased out of the steam-filled room, seeking out his first cup of coffee. He found Joel sitting at the table, leafing through the paper. "I saved you a cup," he said, not even glancing up.

Drake poured a cup and slowly put it to his lips. His dad liked the strong stuff. The stuff that put hair on your chest. "Do you have any milk?" He pulled open the fridge.

"No."

"Dad. Your fridge is empty. What are you eating?" Drake slammed the door shut and moved to where his dad sat. "Seriously, Dad. What are you eating?"

"Get dressed, boy. Then we'll talk."

Drake gazed down at the white, fluffy towel. He looked around for his shorts.

Without raising his eyes from the paper, Joel said, "If you're looking for your shorts, I hung them up on the door in the bedroom. I took the liberty of tossing them in the dryer with one of those frilly smelling fabric sheets."

HIS HANDS WERE CLAMMY, and his heart was racing a bit. Ruby made him feel like some lovestruck teen. He quietly chuckled as he recalled their last evening together. A little tipsy, with her hair dipping into her eyes, her turned-up smile, and bright red cheeks. The warmth of her hand in his, melting his heart inch by inch. He turned to his dad who was gazing out the car window. "I really like Ruby."

"I know."

"I don't know what to do about the long-distance thing. I was thinking about maybe moving to the beach."

His dad shot him a wild look, then turned his attention back to the view out his window.

"Maybe I could get a cottage on the beach, and you and I be roommates."

Joel grunted.

"I know you want your independence and all, Dad, but you are getting up there in years. Wouldn't you like to spend them with me?"

Another wild-eyed look came from Joel. This time bringing a smile to Drake's face.

"Just think it over."

When they pulled into Ruby's lot, she must have seen them through her window because she jogged out to meet them. She popped open the back door and climbed in. "I saw y'all so thought I'd help by coming out. Good morning, Joel." She reached over and patted him on the shoulder. "Good morning, Drake." Her voice dipped into the sexy range and set him on high alert.

Joel growled. "Any morning I get up is a good morning, Ruby."

"Now, now, Joel. Let's be positive."

"Oh, I am. I'm absolutely positive any morning I get up is a good morning." He cracked a smile.

They drove to the café a few minutes over the bridge. Drake ordered pancakes, Joel ordered fried eggs with a side of grits, and Ruby ordered French toast with bacon. Over a much milder cup of coffee, Drake started the conversation.

"I asked Dad to be roomies with me. He's not interested." Drake cocked his head toward Joel.

"I didn't say I wasn't interested. I just didn't respond."

"Do wild-eyed looks count?" Drake playfully bumped Joel's shoulder.

"It would be nice to have Drake close by."

"Thank you, Ruby." Drake tipped his head.

"I know I'd like to see him more often." She flashed a smile and batted her lashes at Drake while Joel wasn't looking.

"My eyesight might be a bit off, and my hearing isn't as sharp as it used to be, but I'm sharp as a tack, and I know what you two are up to." Joel spooned his grits, shoving them into his mouth.

Drake and Ruby laughed so hard she almost choked on her food. "You got us, Joel. We can't hide anything from you."

"So did you make enough money to save Shady Grove Place? That's what I want to know first and foremost before I think about moving."

Ruby leaned in closer. "We did. In fact, after breakfast, I'm meeting Mr. Jensen at Shady Grove Place to tell him the good news. To date, we've collected forty thousand dollars."

Drake picked up his head. "Really? That much?"

"Yes. After I counted everything, a late donation came in. This morning. Some wealthy guy who owns one of the beach houses down on the end of the strip. He donated twenty-five thousand dollars. He said he drives by Shady

Grove Place all the time and has been appalled by the slow deterioration of it. He also said we can count on him for more!" Her eyes lit up the entire table with her enthusiasm.

Joel put his spoon down. "Well this changes everything."

"How so, Dad?"

"Why should I move from my comfortable little apartment, especially after it goes through this transformation?"

Drake sighed.

Ruby twisted her mouth and shrugged.

No one could compete with that last statement, so they just dug in and finished their breakfast.

RUBY HELPED Joel out of the car while Drake got the walker out of the trunk.

"I don't know why I need that thing," Joel growled.

"It helps you, Joel, to stay steady, have balance. You wouldn't want to fall. Things don't mend the way they do in—"

"In young people?" he said, cutting her off flatly.

She drew in a deep breath and counted to three. "Just thinking about you is all." She rested a hand on his back while he trailed off in his walker.

"Man, he's stubborn," Ruby whispered to Drake.

"You can say that again."

Once inside, Joel kept moving his walker toward his apartment. "Gotta use the little boys' room," he called out, making everyone in ear distance smirk.

"Good morning, Mrs. Parker. Is Mr. Jensen here yet?"

"Yes. He's outside looking over the grounds. He's with some eccentric old guy."

Drake and Ruby took a seat at a large round table that some of the residents used for crafting and puzzles. One puzzle had been started. Ruby picked up a piece and inserted it, leaning back and eyeing more of them. Without warning, a loud ruckus came from the back area.

Ruby made eye contact with the fellow and slid out her chair immediately.

"Ruby. I understand you know Peter," Mr. Jensen said.

"Yes, we met today."

"He's been touring the place," Mr. Jensen said, adjusting the collar of his polo shirt.

"Oh?" Ruby replied.

"I just thought about it after I left your place. Maybe if I had a little tour, I could see better where my money would be best served. Looks like the apartments need a refresh, new carpet in here, some paint, maybe some new furnishings, like a big-screen television, and one area I think would best be served is getting that dining facility back up and running. Old people shouldn't be using stoves."

Ruby laughed. Old people. He was right up there with the residents of Shady Grove Place.

"That will take a lot of money, Peter." Ruby rested her hand on Drake's shoulders.

He pushed his chair back and stood next to Ruby. "All of these ideas are great, but many of them are grandiose, wouldn't you say?"

"Why do you say that?" Peter asked, narrowing his eyes.

"I'm just doing a quick calculation, and I'd say what you're proposing could cost upward of one hundred thousand dollars."

"I'm looking for a great tax deduction for this year. Let's do it." Peter crossed his arms and rocked back on his heels. "You get the bids for the work to be done, forward the contracts to my lawyer, and we'll get them paid as they complete the work. I would suggest we get these apartments refurbished first so we can get them filled. Then we can work on the other stuff. I'm glad to see the pool has been repaired. I'd like to see some nice patio furniture, maybe a few cabanas to get out from the sun, that sort of thing."

Ruby's eyes glazed over, and her mind was one foggy mess inside. Everything was happening so fast.

Drake nudged her.

"Yes. Of course. We'll work on that right away."

"Good. I need to have most of the work done by the end of the year. You know for tax purposes." He turned and reached his hand out to Mr. Jensen.

"Nice meeting you," he said, then he left through the front door, leaving them all standing with their jaws agape.

"Sorry, I had to make a little detour," Joel said, coming up behind them. "What happened? Did someone die?"

"No. Uh. It's just that Peter…just donated a bunch more money to Shady Grove Place," Ruby said, her voice decreasing in pitch as she spoke.

"Ruby, don't you have something for Mr. Jensen," Drake said.

Ruby wiggled her eyes and batted her lashes a few times, forcing herself to come back to reality. "Yes." She handed a thick envelope over to him. "Most of it is cash. There are a few checks too. Payable to you. It's more than enough to pay the back taxes. See, this morning I got a visit from Peter as I'm sure he told you. But what I think he failed to mention is his thoughtful donation of twenty-five thousand dollars." She tipped her chin toward the envelope. "It's in there."

Mr. Jensen held the envelope firmly, then tossed it over and over in his hands. He lifted it as if to feel the weight of all this money, realizing it was also lifting a heavy weight off his shoulders. "I couldn't have done this without your help, Ruby. I was ready to turn it over to the bank. I'm thankful you stepped in when you did. You saved Shady Grove Place." He stepped forward and hugged her.

Ruby blinked back the emotions that tried to well up in her eyes. One or two little tears got away, trailing down her face and neck. One tear bobbled near the corner of her mouth. She slipped her tongue out and caught the salty taste of her joyful tears.

"I'm happy to have been able to help. But there's much to be done. I need to start contacting contractors today."

"I need a nap. All of this happiness, tears, and a full belly has me feeling a bit tired." Joel picked up his walker and turned it toward the hall.

Drake reached out for Ruby's hand. She laced her fingers with his, giving her a jolt of emotion that tightened her chest.

"I'm off to deposit this money, then bright and early Monday morning a visit to the tax office. I'll be in touch.

You kids have a great day." Mr. Jensen waved as he stepped out of the building.

At that moment, they heard quiet sobs coming from the reception area. Ruby shrugged, walking over to the counter with Drake right behind her. There, Mrs. Parker sat at a desk with her face in her hands, crying.

"Mrs. Parker. What's the matter?" Ruby asked.

Mrs. Parker looked up, her face a big red blotch, her eyes swollen slits, and wads of Kleenex nearby. "That's the most beautiful thing I've ever heard." She cupped her face and began sobbing again.

Ruby shot a look to Drake, and Drake held her hand. They stood in silence as they watched Mrs. Parker cry.

"Okay, I gotta go," Drake said, breaking the moment of silence.

"Wait. I need a ride home," Ruby said, pulling Drake back from the counter. "Have a great day, Mrs. Parker," they both called out as they ran for the door.

"Oh sure. Leave me in my moment of sadness," Mrs. Parker yelled.

"Don't be sad. Be glad." Drake ducked out the door, laughing and dragging Ruby behind. Once they got outside, he walked her backward up against the wall. He reached up and tucked her hair behind her ear. "You were great in there."

"Thank you," she said.

He leaned in and kissed her.

She closed her eyes as she savored his kiss. He was thanking her. She should be thanking him. His kisses were delightful and should be outlawed.

"I meant it when I said I want to move closer to the beach. I don't know when or how, but I plan to do it." He pulled her hand into his, and her heart fell to her knees.

"We have a lot to do to get this place in shape. Especially before the end of the year. Maybe your dad will recon-sider moving in with you. I'll be here no matter what." She tugged at his hands and dragging them to her chest, she kissed them.

He drew his hands out of her hold. Wrapping his arm around her shoulder, they strolled to his car. She snuggled into him, breathing him in. This. This is what she'd been waiting for.

AFTER HE SAID goodbye to her at the steps, he apologized for having to get back to Orlando.

"I wish I could stay here with you all day, but I gotta get back to Orlando." He stepped down the stairs backward, missing the bottom step and landing a bit off-balance.

"Be careful," she called out.

"I enjoyed this entire weekend. I hope we have many more." The way her eyes twinkled made him want to run up the steps and grab her in a hold, devouring her mouth.

"I had a great time too. Hurry back." She winked.

First the twinkling of her eyes and now the wink. That set him on fire. He ran up the steps and grabbed her, finding her mouth in a hungry desire he didn't even know he was worthy of. Her lips tasted of syrup from her breakfast, and the sweetness made him hungrier for her.

"OKAY," she said, breathing hard and resting her hand on his chest.

"It's hard for me to leave you. I just want to stay wrapped up in your arms all day long. I want to hear the ocean roar in at night while we gaze at dancing flames out there." He turned toward her outdoor fire ring. "I want to cover your shoulders with a blanket and huddle underneath it with you as the night cools. I want all of that and more."

Ruby stood speechless. No man ever had said these words to her. Never. Ever. She tried to speak but the words got shot back down, and instead of speaking, a tightness grew in her throat and tears welled up. She quickly swatted them away. This was no time for tears. She cupped his face and leaned in, kissing him with all the passion she could gather. She didn't want him to leave either.

CHAPTER 16

"Good morning, Mrs. Parker," Ruby said, raising her voice over all the commotion.

"Good morning," she yelled back, cupping her mouth for dramatic effects.

Ruby sidled up to the reception counter. "I know. It's a bit noisy but just think, when this is all done it will be so beautiful."

"I can't wait. Have you seen the apartments?"

"No. Show me."

Mrs. Parker grabbed her key ring and headed toward the hall. Ruby and Red followed behind. When Mrs. Parker pushed open the door, Ruby gasped. It was beautiful.

"Oh my. This is lovely," she said, running her hand along the new kitchen cabinets and countertops.

"The carpet is so cushiony too." Mrs. Parker slid her shoe through the carpet pile and tapped it for good measure.

The smell of new permeated the entire place. From new cabinets and countertops, new tile and fixtures in the bathroom to new paint.

"I love how they chose neutral colors," Ruby said.

"They have only two more to complete. I've already started taking applications," Mrs. Parker sang.

Ruby tried to push away the joyful tears that sought to emerge. She took in a deep breath. "I've been getting updates from Mr. Jensen. Seems the dining facility is the last thing to be overhauled."

"They've just started gutting it. I saw the appliance package they are going to order. Top-of-the-line stuff," Mrs. Parker said, closing up the apartment.

Ruby stood back as Mrs. Parker secured the apartment. "I think that could be the selling point of this place. Having your meals prepared is essential for older people. Proper nutrition, a social place to gather, it's all very important for the well-being of our older residents."

"Are you sure you're a romance author? You sure could be a shrink or something." Mrs. Parker trudged off to the front area.

"Well, writing is like a catch-all profession. I'm constantly doing research for my books. And, I did graduate with a degree in sociology."

"That's nice," Mrs. Parker said, not paying attention, humming as she strolled.

"Speaking of romance…"

"Do tell," Mrs. Parker said with her elbows leaning on the counter.

"Drake and I are getting along. I think he's the one." She shrugged as a wide smile broadened her face.

"Oh. I thought you were going to tell me something else. Everyone within five miles around knows you and Drake are an item." She pulled her elbows up and smirked.

"Oh, really? I thought we'd been kind of low-key about it all." Ruby twisted her lips.

Mrs. Parker shooed her with her hands. "Low-key? Nope. Everyone here knew it."

"Anyway, I just wanted to pop in and see how things were going. I'm headed back home to finish my book."

"Lovely, dear. Enjoy," Mrs. Parker said, turning her back and fidgeting with something.

SHE WAS on his mind almost every minute of the day. He found it difficult to concentrate on his workload. He had to prepare a case for trial, and with Ruby weighing so heavily on his mind, he wondered how he would accomplish it.

Sliding his chair back, he stood and stretched. A cup of coffee might put some zing in his day. He wandered down the corridor of the office and made his way into the lounge area where they sometimes interviewed clients. He made a cup of coffee and then sat, looking through a travel magazine someone had left behind.

"Good morning, Drake."

Drake peered up. It was Skip, the senior partner of the firm and his boss. "Good morning."

"Why don't you head on down to my office in a few. I have something to discuss with you."

Drake pursed his lips. Was he in some sort of trouble? "Sure. I'll be right there."

He topped off his coffee and then as he made his way to Skip's office, he conjured up a lot of excuses as to why he'd been delayed in his responses to his clients.

Ruby. Ruby. Ruby. Would that fly? Probably not.

He rapped on the door once, then pushed it open. Skip sat behind his desk. "Come on in. Close the door."

Close the door.

"What is it you wanted to talk to me about?" Drake cut right to the chase.

The man, dressed in an expensive suit, who he'd known for a few years, played golf with, threw a few cold ones back with, now looked a bit troubled. He chewed on his bottom lip for a few seconds, sending Drake's anxiety level through the roof.

"I know I've been a bit behind with my workload. I can explain."

"No, it's nothing like that Drake. We're pleased with your work. No, I have an opportunity for you. A prestigious law firm in Charleston, South Carolina has an opening. I know the senior partner. We went to law school together. It's a perfect opportunity to get our foot in another state. And since you are our only attorney who took the Uniform Bar Examination, you'd be a perfect fit."

"I see. Charleston, you say?"

"It's a beautiful old city steeped in rich history. Close to the beach, nightlife, and restaurants. I think you'd really like it there."

"My father is my only concern. I'd just been thinking about moving closer to him."

"Maybe he could move with you. Charleston is very senior friendly."

"True."

"Is there anything else holding you back? You broke up with…"

"Chrissy."

"You're essentially unattached. Except for your dad, of course." Skip chuckled.

"It's a lot to think about. When do I have to have an answer?" He slowly stood, smoothing out and pulling taut the sleeves of his suit jacket.

"Well, that's the other thing. It's not really an option, Drake. It's take the job or be out of one." Skip looked him straight in the eyes.

Drake reared his head back. "Seriously? You're firing me?"

"No, not at all. We hope you'll take the position in Charleston. We're downsizing here, is all." He walked around the desk and extended his hand. "Think of it as you were chosen for this and be happy. Take the job, Drake. Don't think about it for too long. Lawyers are a dime a dozen, especially in this town. I think you'd rather be working than not." He shook Drake's hand.

Drake walked back to his office in a daze. Had he heard him correctly? Downsize, Charleston, move. It was all too much to take in. He dropped into his desk chair and slumped forward, resting his elbows on the desk. He cupped his face as the words bounced around in his head. *Charleston. Moving. Leaving Ruby.*

Leaving Ruby!

WITH RED CURLED at the base of the couch, Ruby pulled her laptop onto her lap and began plucking away at the keyboard. The words were flowing, and with each strike of a key, more pulsed through her head onto the computer screen. She blew a strand of hair out of her face as she rushed to make her word count. Leaning back, she read her words. She hit the delete button, typed a few more words, then read the passage again. A big smile crossed her face.

She put the laptop on the coffee table and moved over to the kitchen. She opened the fridge and peeked inside. Nothing looked appetizing to her. She rummaged through her "snack" cabinet, finding an old package of Oreos. She took a little bite. Stale but not awful. She dumped a few onto a plate, poured herself a glass of milk and headed back into her writing cave.

Like a kid, she twisted the cookie apart, licking the white, sugary filling. She licked her fingers clean before she started typing again. When she got to the romantic kiss part, she typed fast and furious as she recalled her own steamy kisses with Drake.

Her phone started jumping all over the table as it vibrated, letting her know she was getting a call. Licking her last two fingers, she grabbed it. *Drake!*

With her legs crossed and a coy smile plastered on her face, she greeted him with her most sexy tone. "Hey there," she said.

"Hey. Listen. I have something really important to discuss with you. Can I see you tonight?"

She pulled her head back when his businesslike tone hit her smack in the face. She decided to play her cards safe, to make sure she wasn't jumping to conclusions. "Sure. That'll be fine," she said calmly.

"Okay. I'll see you then."

She tossed the phone back onto the table. Something about that call didn't ring right to her. His tone was not just businesslike. He had bad news.

DRAKE TRIED LEAVING his apartment on three occasions to go see her. Each time he turned back around. What would he say to her? How would he say it? She wasn't going to believe a word he ever spoke again after tonight. He closed his eyes, drawing in a deep breath. Opportunities like this only come along once in a lifetime.

HER STOMACH WAS TIED up in tiny knots as she waited for him. This wasn't their normal date or hanging out that they did. No, something was brewing, and Ruby had no idea what it could be. *Maybe it was Joel? That's it. Something bad has happened with Joel.*

She tried to busy herself by cleaning. She scoured the shower, got on her hands and knees and washed the bathroom floor, and spit shined the mirror over the sink. She rearranged her sock and underwear drawer, lined her shoes according to style and color in her closet and tossed away all the expired stuff from inside her fridge. A light rap on her front door alerted Red. She already knew it was him. She heard his car drive up.

"Hey," she said, opening the door. She waited for the kiss, but he walked right through the door.

She shut the door with a swift push of her hand. "No kiss? This really must be bad news?" She placed her hands on her hips, eyeing him deeply.

He'd already made himself at home. He patted the cushion next to him. "I need to talk to you."

She begrudgingly sat next to him, her arms now crossed, and she sported a major pout.

He rested his hand on her knee. "You know I care about you a lot, right?" He tipped his head to urge her to agree.

She tossed darts from her hurt eyes.

"Ruby. Seriously. This isn't easy for me. But it's a once-in-a-lifetime opportunity."

She pulled her crossed arms tighter across her chest.

"I have an opportunity to move to Charleston, South Carolina and become a partner in a very old and prestigious law firm."

Her eyes flew open, her arms dropped, and tears brimmed under her lids.

"I think I need to take it."

"You think you have to take it? What about Joel?"

"I know. I've thought about it. He has to come with me. He'll love Charleston."

"Drake. Do you hear yourself? In five minutes, not even five, you've broken up with me, taken a job in Charleston and moved your dad out of the one place he loves."

He reached for her, but she pulled away.

"I mean, did you really think this through? What happened to I want to move to the beach?" Her voice was condescending, and she hoped it cut through him like a knife.

"It's one of the hardest things I've ever done. I wanted to stay. See where this thing went between us. But I'm still young, and my career is very important. I hoped you would understand."

"I understand quite well. Thanks for coming by. I wish you a lot of luck in Charleston. When are you leaving?"

"Next week."

"Next week. That's sudden. Poor Joel won't know what hit him."

"I can come back for him after I get settled in."

"That would be better. At least you're thinking clearly regarding that."

Leaning over to pat Red on the head, he scratched him behind the ears "I hope we can still be friends." He walked over to the front door.

She was dying inside. She held her tears at bay as he bid her farewell. Then tipping his head one last time, he was gone.

The tears came in buckets. She'd held them as long as she could. He'd not even driven away yet. She could see the beams of his headlights as he tore out of her driveway. *How could he do this to us?*

Us. Us. Us.

CHAPTER 17

Drake had been gone for two weeks. She hadn't heard from him since he came over that night to give her the news. He'd chosen a new job over her. The grand reopening of Shady Grove Place was scheduled for the following week. Thanks to Mrs. Parker and her dedication, Shady Grove Place was now at full occupancy. Of course, they were going to have a vacancy soon when Joel moved out. Joel hadn't said too much about moving to Charleston. Ruby stayed clear of the subject anyway. It was still too raw. She thought about Drake all the time.

"Hi, Joel." Ruby sat next to him as they both enjoyed the early sunshine that peeked over the trees.

"Hello."

"How are you?"

"Fine."

Red moved closer to Joel so he could get his ears scratched.

Joel didn't reach out to Red. Red wagged his tail, then looked at Ruby.

"Joel, Red says hello." Ruby rubbed Red's head since Joel wasn't going to.

Joel hmphed.

"Joel, it doesn't help to be mean to us."

Us. Us. Us.

"We didn't do anything. We're here for you." She stood. "If you ever need anything, anything at all, just call me."

"Ruby," he said.

Ruby whirled around. "Yes, Joel."

"I'm mad at him."

She sat back down.

"I'm mad because he didn't discuss it with me before he did it. I don't want to move."

"I know, Joel. It was rather sudden."

"Sudden? That's mild. More like I can't breathe."

Ruby patted him on the leg. "I know it seems overwhelming now, but let Drake work things out. We don't really know what's happening. I haven't heard from him." She hung her head.

"That's another thing. What a dumb-ass. I mean, what's he thinking? I'll tell you what he's thinking. He's not!"

"Thank you for caring about me so much. I'll be all right. These things happen." She stood again. "Have a great day, Joel."

She greeted a few more residents, then made her way back inside. Mrs. Parker was giving information at the front desk to a couple interested in moving there. Ruby smiled. Boy how things had changed.

DRAKE MET the new partners at the law firm. They were nice enough. But things were a bit more uptight in Charleston. The attorneys were slow-speaking older gentlemen, and if suits alone showed worth, Drake figured each of them were filthy rich. He rented a room at an extended stay hotel. He really wasn't in a hurry to find an apartment. He preferred to get to know his surroundings before that. It'd been two weeks since he left Orlando. He wondered if Ruby would take a call from him. But first, he'd call his dad and feel him out. Surely Ruby had been to visit him by now.

"Hey, Dad. How are you?" He tried to keep his voice happy and positive.

"I'm fine."

"Good. Good. Charleston is a very pretty little town. Lots of history here. After you move here, we can check out all the historical stuff, okay?"

"I don't want to move there, Drake. How many times do I have to tell you?"

"I know, Dad. But I'm worried about leaving you there. What if something happens?"

"Charleston is not that far away. If I'm in the hospital, you still have time to come see me, and if I'm dead, well it won't matter if you live in Orlando or Charleston, will it?"

Drake sighed. "True."

"Besides, Ruby said she'd look in on me."

"Ruby?"

"Yes. Ruby. Remember her? The pretty little girl you left behind for Charleston." His voice was angry, and Drake took notice.

"It was one of the hardest things I've ever done, Dad. Of course, I remember Ruby. She's all I think about."

"Well, then why'd you do it? Come back, Son. It's not too late. She still thinks about you."

"How do you know that?"

"I just do."

Drake hung up the phone. Sitting in the dark with no sound and only images of the television illuminating the room, he stared at the screen, void of any feelings, numb from his decision to leave Orlando and the only girl he truly ever loved.

He balled up his fist and punched the nearby pillow. "Why?" he said through gritted teeth.

RUBY WAS thankful she had committed to a book signing in nearby Orlando. She boxed up her books, tossed her box of swag and her easel into her car, grabbed some dog treats for Red and the two hit the road. She sang to the oldies that played from her old radio, trying to make the drive go by faster. Everything went pretty well until she passed the exit to Drake's apartment. Her eyes teared up.

She got to the venue and set up. She tried to be cordial to her author buds. They were happy to see her, so she strived to display a stiff upper lip and not show how devastated she felt. When the fans started pouring in, she soon got lost in the book world, and Drake didn't even pop into her brain.

After the signing, several of the authors went out for Mexican food and margaritas. It was a great time had by all, but when she started on her second margarita, she got loose-lip syndrome and began to tell them all about Drake. Soon everyone was crying.

They walked her to her car with arms draped over her, trying to console her.

"Are you sure you're able to drive home?"

"I'm fine. I've been so emotional over the breakup. I'm sorry I blabbered on about him." She stiffened her back.

"I'm going to stop for a cup of coffee to take with me. But really, I'm okay."

She did as she promised. She stopped and got a giant-sized coffee. She sipped on it as she drove home. She wasn't tipsy as much as she was brokenhearted.

Her phone started playing music, taking her mind off of him. She quickly hit the button to her earbuds. "Hello."

"Hey."

The voice on the other end sent chills up and down her spine, took her breath away, and made her pulse quicken.

"Ruby?"

"Yes," she squeaked out.

"How are you?"

She bit on her lip. *How was she*?

"I talked to Dad a little bit ago."

"Oh?"

"Come on. Please talk to me."

His voice used to make her stomach tie in knots, now it made her skin crawl.

"Okay. I'll let you go. Just wanted to hear your voice."

"Well you heard it. Goodbye."

Click.

She reached over and turned up the radio and began to hum to the oldies, bouncing around in her seat like a crazy person while tears rolled down her cheeks.

CHAPTER 18

*R*uby and Mrs. Parker worked on the article for the local newspaper. With Mr. Jensen's approval, Ruby submitted it for publication. Shady Grove Place was having a party.

She made the rounds to the bakery, asking them to make a beautiful cake. This time they were paying for it. Then she went to the café and sat with the owner, discussing food for the event. Everywhere she went that day, she left happy and also put a smile on someone else's face. What goes around comes around, her grandmother used to say. Satisfied she'd checked all the boxes on her to-do list, Ruby and Red headed home. The one thing she'd been putting off could no longer be put off. A certain manuscript had to be wrapped up, and although the ending would have to change, Ruby was ready to take it on.

For some reason, wine always seemed to help her write. Especially the romantic scenes. But what about breakup scenes? That called for something stronger. She pulled out the bottle of bourbon she'd had forever and poured a shot into a small glass. She dropped her nose over the rim and took a whiff. Notes of sweet coffee, tobacco, and vanilla wafted to her nostrils. She took a sip and rolled it around her tongue, then swallowed it. Rich, balanced between dry and sweet fading quickly. Sort of like her relationship with Drake.

She crossed over to her computer with her drink. This could be the best writing she'd ever done.

The only light came from her monitor and the moon shining through the window. She squinted at her screen. It was two o'clock in the morning. She arched her back and heaved her shoulders, stretching. She stood and stretched some more. She powered down her computer but not before she typed, THE END. Then she stumbled off to bed with Red trailing behind.

"RUBY!" Mr. Jensen called.

"Hi there." Ruby peeped around at the crowd that gathered at Shady Grove Place. The caterers were setting up tables with warming dishes, and some young men the bakery had hired were carefully setting up the cake. Ruby gazed over to the reception desk where Mrs. Parker was arranging a vase of colorful flowers. "The place looks so nice."

"I can't thank you enough for everything you've done to keep Shady Grove a reality. I'd given up a long time ago." He swooped his arm over her shoulders and squeezed her.

"That's quite all right. I looked at is as a rescue of sorts. It was a challenge well accepted."

"I understand you and Drake had a falling out. I'm sorry to hear that. Joel tells me he's taken a job in South Carolina."

Ruby nodded. "And trying to convince Joel to move there too."

"He doesn't want to. Wants me to interfere on his behalf," Mr. Jensen said.

"I wouldn't get involved in family matters, Mr. Jensen. It never bodes well."

"True. Listen, Mrs. Parker has informed me we are at one hundred percent occupancy now."

"Yes, and I'm happy with the chef you hired for the dining room," Ruby said. "He's very educated and well versed in what old people like and don't." She laughed and soon Mr. Jensen joined her.

"So true."

"I think we'll make our rounds and say hi to everyone. Come on, Red."

Ruby shook hands with residents, hugged others, and talked to everyone she laid eyes on. Red ate up the attention. When Ruby caught a glimpse of Joel giving Red a piece of cake, she shrieked. "Joel. Don't please. It will give him diarrhea."

Joel grunted. "A little piece like this?" He held a morsel between his fingers.

"Please don't." She shook her head fervently.

"Have you heard from my no-good son?"

"In fact, I have."

"Oh?"

"He called me, but truthfully, Joel, I didn't have anything to say to him. It was a short conversation."

"He said he might come to this today." Joel peered at her through squinted eyes.

"I wouldn't hold my breath, Joel."

Joel tipped his head and made Ruby look.

Her mouth dropped open when she saw him walk through the door. Dressed in gray cargo-style shorts and a baby blue knit collared shirt tucked in neatly, Drake Carrolton stood front and center, a shy smile crossing his face. He flipped his hand up in a wave and took more steps toward her.

Her heart dropped to her knees, her pulse raced, and her mouth felt as if she'd eaten an entire bag of cotton balls. She swallowed the lump that instantly formed and strained to hear anything clearly over the ringing in her ears. Her vision blurred as he got closer. Was it really him? His gorgeous body moved slowly toward her, exposing every emotion she'd ever felt for him. Right here. At Shady Grove Place for everyone to see.

"Hey."

His sexy voice weaved through her mind. She wanted to run into his arms. Tell him she loved him. But what fool would do a thing like that?

"Hey."

"I hope you aren't angry for me showing up."

She shook her head.

"I wanted to tell you, but you hung up on me."

She nodded.

He stepped closer, then reached for her hands. "Ruby. I'm sorry how we left things. I really am. I was sort of forced to make a decision. One I wasn't ready for. It happened all so fast."

"I didn't ask you to make a decision about us, Drake. I'm sorry if you felt I was giving you an ultimatum. I'd never do that."

He ran his thumb along hers and made the hairs on her arm stand up. "No, not you. My law firm. They gave me an ultimatum. They said take the job in Charleston or find a new one."

"Why didn't you tell me all of that. I'd have understood."

"I know. I guess I got scared. I don't know what happened."

"Maybe you thought we were moving too fast. This was your way out?" Ruby stayed focused on him.

He shook his head. "No. That's not it. At least I don't think it was. I want to be with you. You're all I ever think about. I couldn't concentrate on work in Orlando, and I definitely can't concentrate in Charleston." He pulled her closer.

"What are you saying exactly?" Ruby asked.

"I'm moving back. I told them, as much as I appreciated the opportunity, my heart belongs in Shady Grove. I wouldn't be productive there, and besides, my dad is here." Drake searched for Joel. When he made eye contact, he flashed him a wide smile.

"What about me?" Ruby asked.

He leaned over and kissed her.

Quickly, the crowd erupted in applause. Ruby, red in the face, her pulse quickened by the moment, turned around. There stood Mrs. Parker, Mr. Jensen, and Joel along with some of the long-time residents she'd befriended, smiling, clapping, hollering and kicking up commotion for them.

She mouthed thank you, then turned back to Drake.

"Where are you going to live?"

"It just so happens that a cottage came up for sale just down the beach from you."

"Are you serious?"

"We're going to be neighbors," he said.

Mrs. Parker moved closer to Joel and whispered in his ear. Unfortunately, everyone heard it. She couldn't whisper to save her life. "I bet they move in together. That neighbor thing won't last long," she said, shaking her finger side to side.

Joel widened his eyes. "Hey, I always said I wanted to live on the beach."

"Now, Joel. Don't count your chickens before they hatch."

Drake, Ruby, and the rest of the folks broke out in laughter.

"So, neighbor. How about you come over and partake in a little housewarming party." Drake kissed Ruby again.

Narrowing her eyes, she replied, "Party?"

"Not really a *party* party. More like a little alone time. Just you and me." He crinkled up his nose and started to lean in.

She stopped him with her hand. "Okay, but first, a walk on the beach."

"Take some food," Mr. Jensen said.

They made the rounds, loading up plates with boiled shrimp, olives, cheese, and two big slices of cake. Drake offered to take the filled plates with him since she had Red. They agreed to meet halfway down the beach. She gave him a quick kiss, hurrying home to freshen up.

CHAPTER 19

She followed behind him as they drove the little strip of road that led to the row of beach houses. He continued on, and she drove straight, making a quick turn into her driveway. She and Red rushed inside where she spritzed on some cologne, put on some lip gloss and fluffed up her hair, deciding to toss it into a rubber band instead of leaving it down. She opened the screen door and peered down the sandy beach. She could see a man walking in the distance. It had to be him.

Red followed Ruby until he realized it was Drake and then galloped to meet him. Ruby could hear his chuckle as Red greeted him. The sun was just beginning its descent. It was one of those lazy summer afternoons where the sky wasn't a brilliant blue, but instead, white clouds weaved in and out of the deep blue. The waves softly rolled in, giving just a taste of how the tide would roar in and out later.

He swung his arm around her, pulling her close. "Wait until you see my place."

"I still can't believe something came available. Cottages rarely come for sale here."

Abruptly, they stopped in front of a gray, weather-beaten cottage with a screen door hanging by one hinge. Above the front door, a plaque read, The Sea Breeze. She twirled toward him. "This. This is your place? The Sea Breeze?"

"Uh-huh. Do you know of it?"

"Yes, I do. People along the beach say it's haunted."

"What?" Drake turned and focused on the cottage.

She took a few steps toward the structure. "Yes, apparently an old sea captain used to live here. It's one of the oldest cottages here. I think it was built in—"

"Nineteen forty-two," he said, cutting in.

She blinked a few times. "It's withstood wind, rain, beach erosion, and even a few hurricanes."

"What happened to the sea captain?" Drake asked.

"Legend has it he went out on a boat and never came back. But kids who come out here at night say his ghost can be seen walking from window to window, carrying a lantern."

"Now you're just trying to scare the crap out of me."

She took his hand and walked up to the wooden steps. "I guess the real estate agent didn't tell you about the lore, huh?" She ascended the steps, each one wobbling under her weight.

"I have to fix those," he said, eyeing the dry-rotted wood.

"You might want to contact someone to get rid of the ghost." She reached for the doorknob.

"Wait."

She turned.

"I don't know if I want to go inside again."

"You're not afraid of some old ghost, are you?" She tilted her head.

"I just wish you'd not told me about it, is all." He pushed open the door, motioning for her to step inside first.

He immediately began flicking on lights. Soon every room in the small cottage was lit up like a Christmas tree.

She took in the shabby details of the rugged cottage. Threadbare curtains, overstuffed chairs, and a musty smell. It could use some refreshing. She sat on the couch. "Come here."

He eased down onto the sofa. Every time he heard a noise, he focused toward it. She noticed his chest rising and falling with each anxious move he made. She began to giggle.

"What's so funny? I don't think this is funny one bit. I've bought a house with a ghost in it. I think this is grounds to sue the agent. Shouldn't she have to disclose this?" He leaned back with his arms crossed.

"Drake Carrolton. Are you always this gullible?" She stared at him openmouthed.

His eyes grew to the size of saucers. "Ruby Bennett. Were you pulling my leg about the ghost?" He reached for her, dropping her onto his lap.

She reached up and laced her hands around his neck.

"I should have known you were tricking me." He gasped, covering his mouth. "No, please don't," he shrieked, his eyes bugging out of his head.

Ruby's heart plummeted as she jumped off his lap, facing the door where his eyes froze.

"What! What is it, Drake?" She looked around the room.

He started bellowing so hard that he fell off of the couch onto the floor. Ruby caught on quickly.

"Drake!" She play-slapped his arm.

He covered his face and laughed some more. His words muffled by his hands, she pried them away so she could understand him.

"I knew you were messing with me about the ghost right off the bat. I got you good."

She whirled around, crossing her arms at her chest.

He lifted himself up off the floor and turned her around. He mimicked the pout she had on her face. "Are you mad at me?" He leaned in and kissed her.

"Sort of."

"What can I do to make it up to you?" He pulled her hands out of her arm-hug and laced his fingers with hers. "I'm sorry."

"You better not ever scare me like that again. I really thought some ax man or something was standing at the door. The horrid look on your face was real."

"Let's start over. Welcome to Sea Breeze where ghosts do not live, but a sea captain did, as you well know, the basis of your trumped-up story. It needs a little work, but I think it will be fine. I like the close proximity to the beach and Dad."

"What about the close proximity to me and Red? Speaking of Red. Where is he?"

Drake ran to the door and opened it. On the porch, curled up in a tight ball, eyes wide open was Red on duty.

"Ah. He's protecting us from the boogeyman." She looped her arm around his waist. The tide was rolling in, and the sounds of the waves were like music to her ears. "We have to fix up this porch."

"All in good time, Ruby. All in good time."

"Hey. You never told me, what are you going to do now that you've moved to the beach? I'm not aware of any law offices here."

"Excellent question. I'm going to open my own business. I'm going to start by offering legal aid at a discount to the seniors of Shady Grove Place to help prepare wills and that sort of thing, and I had some cool business cards made up that I was hoping you'd help me hand out. I can provide legal services to anyone who may need them."

"Will that be enough to pay the bills?"

"It's a start. I have some other ideas up my sleeve that we can discuss at a later date."

She leaned back against his hold and stared deep into his eyes. "I never knew I could be so happy. You came into my life at the right time."

"I feel the exact same way. I was so done with women after Chrissy, but then I met you and everything I ever thought I knew about women went crashing out into the ocean."

"We make a great team." She reeled herself in closer to him, their chests touching lightly.

"You can say that again." He lowered his head and paused before kissing her. "Are you going to write about us in your next book?"

She posed for the kiss. "You can bet on it."

He lowered his mouth to hers and kissed her as the waves came booming in on the beach.

Every morning like clockwork, they'd meet halfway in the middle. She'd give him a cup of coffee she'd brewed, and they'd walk in silence, enjoying the morning quiet of the beach. Often times she'd be going over plot ideas in her head while Drake would run with Red and play catch with him. After their morning routine, they'd walk back to the middle, kiss each other bye and walk back to their respective cottages.

She'd work on her writing, and he'd go to work drafting wills and other legal documents. It worked out great, and he understood well her commitment to writing.

Joel dropped an idea on them one day while over for dinner at Ruby's.

"I don't know why you two just don't get married. Seems ridiculous you are down there and she is up here."

"Dad, we're quite happy with our arrangement," Drake said.

"Yes, Joel. We have the best of both worlds," Ruby said.

"I don't get it. You young people." Joel shook his head. "I'm not going to be around forever. I'd like to see you two tie the knot."

"Dad, are you feeling poorly?"

"No, I just would like to see you guys get married."

"Joel, we can't just get married because you think it's the best idea," Ruby said, clearing the plates from the table.

"Don't you love each other?"

Ruby stood frozen as she held the dishes. Love. Neither one of them had ever spoken the three words.

"Dad. That's a bit personal, don't you think?" Drake rested his hand on the back of Joel's chair, looking up at Ruby.

Ruby turned and moved into the kitchen and began rinsing the dishes. Drake came up behind her, his hands resting just at her hips. He whispered in her ear, "I love you."

She stood frozen again, unable to move. She batted her lashes a few times and then slowly turned into his arms, now facing him.

"Drake, you don't—"

He held up a finger and pressed it to her lips. "Shh."

"I know you care about me. You don't have to tell me that," she said, her pitch wavering.

"I know I don't have to. I want to. I've wanted to say it for a long time. I've been a little worried about how you'd take it."

"I'll admit I don't want anything to change between us. I love it just the way it is. So many times, the words love and marriage change things in a relationship. I don't want that for us." Her eyes began to well with tears.

"Don't cry. This isn't meant to make you sad or question anything. I just saw the look on your face when Dad said what he said. It prompted me to tell you. But we can keep things the way they are. I'm good with that too." He held her hands and squeezed them.

"I've been alone for so long. No parents, siblings, or even a boyfriend. It's just been me and Red…and my writing." Her bottom lip trembled. "I do love you, though. I just was scared to say it."

"Scared like when I pretended an ax murderer was standing at my door?"

"Scared like when you thought a ghost lived at your cottage," she said, nodding.

They both started to laugh so hard that Ruby snorted, Red started barking, and Joel hollered from the other room.

"I told you guys you belong together. Now get married!"

Ruby and Drake held hands as they walked into the tiny living room. Joel was sitting in a rocker, Red at his feet.

Drake looked over to Ruby, and when she gave him the go-ahead, he gazed back to his dad.

"You'll be happy to know…"

"What, Son, what?" Joel sat forward in the chair, his gaze darting from Ruby back to Drake.

"You just got yourself a beach cottage."

Joel started rocking and laughing. "Hear that, Red. I got myself a beach cottage."

Drake leaned over and kissed Ruby. Life was complete for them both, and finally Ruby had her happily ever after ending just like she'd written about a hundred times.

If you're ready to go to the next book in the series, follow the link for Montana Miracle. Happy Reading!

ABOUT THE AUTHOR

A USA Today bestselling author, Debbie writes sweet contemporary romance and women's fiction. She currently lives on the east coast with her husband and dachshund rescue, Dash. She loves to hike, work in the garden, and on most sunny days you can find her enjoying her backyard. She's an avid supporter of animal rescue, and as such, pledges to happily donate a percentage of all book sales to local and national rescue organizations. When you purchase any of her books, you're also helping animals.

To find out more about Debbie, check out her website at https://www.authordebbiewhite.com

Perfect Pitch

Ties That Bind

Passport To Happiness

The Missing Ingredient

The Salty Dog

The Pet Palace

Billionaire Auction

Billionaire's Dilemma

Coaching the Sub

Christmas Romance – Short Stories